"That the author waited 50 years to say goodbye to his father turns out to be our good fortune. This is a long, beautiful ride in the country."

David Paul Lyday, author/screenwriter

"A lilting tale about life in small-town America. The stories are both touching and funny, but, most of all, filled with love for the man named Jud."

Ann Stingle, playwright

Letters to Jud

Stories of Another Life

Don Alderman

iUniverse, Inc.
Bloomington

Letters to Jud
Stories of Another Life

This is a work of fiction. Experiences described, while fictionalized, were
inspired by actual occurrences. The names of several actual persons have
been used, but a number of the individuals portrayed are composites of more
than one person and many names and identifying characteristics
have also been changed.

iUniverse books may be ordered through booksellers or by contacting:

iUniverse
1663 Liberty Drive
Bloomington, IN 47403
www.iuniverse.com
1-800-Authors (1-800-288-4677)

ISBN: 978-1-4401-8135-1 (sc)
ISBN: 978-1-4401-8137-5 (hc)
ISBN: 978-1-4401-8136-8 (e)

Printed in the United States of America

iUniverse rev. date: 09/02/2011

For who else but Colleen,
whose belief and encouragement
kept this project alive.

Contents

Goodbye. 1

The Old Dodge. 9

The Firefly 16

Little Sir Echo 24

Folklore 34

Ghosts 43

Listening to Screen Doors 50

Life and Death Matters. 54

The Chicken Killers. 60

The Weezer Bug 65

The Art of Eddie Byers. 69

Haunting Ida. 76

Spider Hunting 80

Saving Gauze. 86

The Vegetable Man 94

Christmas Eve 100

A Little Night Music. 104

My Meeting with the President 113

Woody Blossoms 122

Bad Apples. 127

Marshal Law 139

Bawdy Language 152

My Brief Movie Career 163

Depot's End 175

Thoughts on Letters to Jud. 187

Sweet childish days, that were as long as twenty days are now.

— William Wordsworth

*The happy highways where I went
And cannot come again.*

— A. E. Housman

Goodbye

Dear Jud:

Let me begin by saying goodbye. I didn't get a chance to do that on the morning I left Republic to go to Texas.

That isn't exactly true. I did have that chance, but I didn't take it. My suitcase was in the trunk of my green Plymouth, and you and I and Isabel were standing in the dining room trying to say our parting words. You were about to leave for the depot, as you'd done for nearly fifty years, and you were telling me to have a safe trip and to be very careful. I wanted to respond but wasn't able. The words were too thick and tight in my throat, and I feared the sound that might come out if I opened my mouth.

You looked at me for just a moment, wondering, I'm sure, if I was going to say anything. Then you gave me a small smile as you put on your familiar brown fedora, and you left through the front door. In a moment, through the dining room window, I saw the blue Nash heading west on Elm Street as you drove toward the depot.

I left soon afterward. When I mumbled "Bye" to Isabel, my voice sounded high and strained. Her own parting words were understated, and I suspect that my difficulty with goodbyes may have been inherited from her. She stood in the doorway of the front porch as I got into my car. I started the engine, and when I looked up to wave at her, she was watching me with a fixed expression. She gave a small wave in reply.

Initially, I drove toward town on Elm Street. But after a couple of blocks, I decided to turn around and drive to the beginning of our street so that I could make one final trip along the old street that had been such an important part of my life. I drove east on Elm until it became a gravel road, and then I turned and headed west again.

Driving slowly, I looked to my right and saw Barney Davis's house. This triggered thoughts of the trips Bob and I had made, as young boys, to pick up baskets of eggs or buckets of milk from the Davises. I remembered, especially, one crisp winter morning—the one on which Bob and I had tried to make milk out of snow.

Isabel had handed us a milk bucket—the flimsy one-gallon aluminum pail used for that purpose—and sent us out to buy milk from Barney Davis. We secured the lid, set the empty pail on our sled, and pulled it through the snow toward the Davises'. Barney had taken milk fresh from the cow in their back lot, and the milk was still warm as he poured it from his big bucket into our gallon pail. We replaced the lid, handed him the money Isabel had given us, put the pail on our sled, and started toward home. On the trip back, I was pulling the sled through the icy ruts in the snow. Bob said I was walking too slowly and pushed the back of the sled with his foot. The sled shot forward and rammed painfully into the tendon above my heel. Enraged, I grabbed the aluminum bucket by its wire handle and swung the heavy container in an arc that ended at the top of Bob's head. The lid burst off and milk sprayed through the cold winter air, settling invisibly into the snow.

The impact of the lightweight pail hadn't hurt Bob, but his head had produced a large dent in one side of the pail. When we looked into the pail we saw that more than half of the contents had been spilled. We thought about that. We thought about arriving home with a half-empty bucket. And we thought about a now-urgent need to have some explanation that Isabel would accept. Nothing came to mind—until one of us observed that both milk and snow are white.

We punched the inside of the bucket until the dent was barely visible and the rim was nearly circular again. Then, with our wet leather mittens, we scooped snow into the milk until a whitish slush nearly filled the pail. We forced the lid back on, placed the container on the sled and delivered the mixture to Isabel. The condition of the bucket must have alerted her. I was surprised to see how quickly she deduced that the white stuff wasn't milk, but

I wasn't surprised when she sent us to the cellar stairs, where we sat in exile without lunch for a good part of the day.

The Plymouth was entering our block, so I slowed to take a final look at our house, and fix its familiar features in my mind. Isabel had gone inside.

The rapid bumping of my Plymouth's wheels roused me from that recollection. I realized that I was driving over the "washboard," the rippled stretch of blacktop in front of the Huckins' house. After I learned to drive a car, I noticed for the first time that at certain points, Elm Street's blacktop surface was wavy enough to rattle your teeth. But the pavement wasn't always so corrugated. It was as smooth as velvet for a while after they first paved the street in 1941.

Bob and I had watched the transformation from our front yard. We were there when the Greene County road crews came to scrape and level Elm Street, which was a dirt road at that time. We were fascinated by the strange-looking contraption that followed, extruding thick, smoking, tarry-smelling asphalt over the gravel.

We stood at the edge of the sewer ditch that ran in front of our house, watching the road builders. And they watched us, two barefoot seven-year-old boys wearing identical striped overalls. The men who followed the paving machine and poked around with shovels and other tools would glance at us occasionally and grin. One of them, leaning on the end of his long-handled shovel, asked if we'd like to leave our footprints in the hot tar. We both backed away a couple of steps, which made the men laugh. At noon, several of the road builders took their lunch break under the ash trees in front of our house. I watched them eat from a distance, but Bob sat cross-legged in the grass near them so that he could see what came out of their black lunch pails.

Two of the lunch companions were dump-truck drivers who hauled the gravel. After their meal, while they smoked cigarettes, Bob struck up a conversation. I ventured closer, and soon we had become friends with the drivers. Later that day, Isabel allowed us to take them glasses of ice water, and they reciprocated by inviting us to ride in their trucks to the gravel quarry near Nixa. They said that we could see where gravel came from. Isabel looked them over and decided that it would be safe enough. So, for the next couple of days we rode back and forth with our new friends in their separate trucks when they emptied their loads of gravel on Elm Street and returned to the quarry for more.

Bob's driver was a dark-haired, stocky young man who seemed to enjoy Bob's jokes. His name was Joe. My driver, Jim, was an older man, lean, graying, and kindly. He seemed to understand my shyness and kept the conversation going as we rode together in his truck. He told me that he had a grandson about my age and that his name was Dennis. During a lull in the conversation on one of our trips to Nixa, Jim asked me where we went to church. I told him, "Methodist," and when I asked if he was a Methodist, too, he just laughed and said, "Naw, I'm a pugilist."

I admired the way Jim could steer the dump truck with his left hand while using his right hand to fish a pack of Camels out of his shirt pocket and shake a cigarette out of the package far enough to grasp the end with his lips. After returning the pack to his shirt pocket, he'd take a kitchen match from a box on the seat and ignite the match by flicking the white part of the match head with his stout, rough-edged thumbnail. The match smoke combined with the first puff of cigarette smoke to create a special perfume. Riding along with Jim, summer wind blowing in through my window, I couldn't think of anything that smelled better than the fragrance of a cigarette freshly lit by a kitchen match in the cab of a workman's truck.

After a few days, the gravel-spreading phase of the Elm Street paving project was finished, and Jim and Joe had to move on to another project in another town. I didn't say goodbye to Jim as he looked at me kindly from the cab of his truck. I could only wave. I watched his truck lumber away, but I kept hoping that, somehow, if I didn't say the word it wouldn't truly be goodbye and my friend Jim wouldn't have to go away.

By now, my Plymouth had come abreast of the O'Neal Lumber and Coal Company lumberyard near the end of Elm Street. I glanced right to look at the ancient brick sidewalk that ran beside the lumberyard fence. It was separated from the pavement by a weedy ditch—the same ditch from which Billy Ransom, lying in it drunk, had hailed my sister Patty one night on her way home from town. She was walking carefully along the dark, uneven sidewalk and didn't see Billy, who was resting in the ditch. But he spotted her through the gloom, and, as she hurried away, he invited her, using courtly language, to join him in the ditch for a sip from his bottle. As she hurried on, she could hear the voice from the ditch entreating her to have a little drink.

At the intersection of Elm and Main Street, I turned right and decided to make a final pass through the two-block business district. As I drove past the not-yet-opened grocery stores, post office, hardware store, drug stores and other businesses, it occurred to me that I might not ever do business at these familiar enterprises again. I entered the residential stretch on North Main and turned onto one of the cross streets, intending to make a loop back toward your depot.

I saw the Rohrs' house on my left, and I recalled the day Jess Rohr mistook me for his son. I knew that Jess worked at the Frisco rail yards in Springfield, and I wondered at times why you and he weren't friends, since he also was a Frisco man. I didn't understand then that you and Jess simply had little in common. On that day, he was in his front yard, highly intoxicated, as was often the case, and in that condition his bleary eyes informed him that the boy he saw walking on the sidewalk was his ten-year-old son, Gerald.

He squinted at me and said, "Jer'! C'mere and help me." When I hesitated, he said, "Hurry up! C'mon over here!" I was a child and he was an adult, so I obeyed. Approaching him, I could see Betsy, the Rohrs' female bird dog, lying on her side. Parts of bricks and large rocks were piled on her paws.

Jess swayed and gestured and slurred his words as he explained why he had called me over. He had positioned Betsy's legs in the classic bird dog "point" attitude, with one front leg raised, and was stacking the bricks and rocks on her paws to hold her legs in place. He ordered me to go find more material to use as weights. Even at my young age, this seemed to be an odd way to train a bird dog. Betsy raised her head and rolled her eyes at me, as if to say "Can't you do something?" But she didn't seem to be suffering greatly, so I meekly agreed to help. I walked back to the street to see if I could locate any large rocks along the edge of the blacktop. Finding none, I looked back at Jess, who had wandered away from Betsy, also looking for additional weights. I decided to make my getaway and proceeded toward home. Jess spotted me walking away and shouted "Jer'! C'm back here! Jer'! I'm gonna whip yer ass!" I broke into a run, and dashed down the street until his boozy voice faded away.

My Plymouth and I had returned to the business district, so I turned right and drove south again toward the railroad tracks until I saw the gray depot ahead. I turned onto West Elm and slowed to a stop in the street, just outside the window of your office.

As I glanced into the window, I recalled that it hadn't been so long ago that I had sat at the old desk I could see inside. It had been a summer vacation day after my freshman year in high school, and you had asked me to help you reduce a mountain of paperwork created by heavy freight traffic. There were dozens of boxcar manifests, and information from these needed to be typed onto the freight bills.

You handed me a tall stack of papers and directed me to a typewriter at the extra work desk. I regretted taking that freshman typing class and acquiring that skill which you now wanted me to demonstrate. I felt gloomy as I began to type out the freight bills—original, plus green, pink, and yellow copies, all separated by sheets of carbon paper. After I'd completed several of the forms I stared, feeling trapped and without hope, out the window.

Across the street at French Chevrolet, I saw a car pull up to the Cities Service gasoline pumps. Three men were in the front seat. As I watched, the driver and the man on the far side got out and slammed their doors, leaving the third man still inside.

The two men walked to the entrance of the dealership's showroom, and, as soon as they entered, the man in the car leaned toward the driver-side door, opened it, and sprawled onto the gravel driveway. He got to his feet, staggered around the front of the car and began to make his way toward the showroom. The other two men must have spotted him, because they came outside and wrestled the third man through the car door on the passenger side. Inside the car, the third man quickly scrambled across the seat on his hands and knees, opened the driver's door, and fell headfirst onto the gravel again. His companions ran around the car, helped him to his feet, walked him to the other side of the car, and shoved him inside again. And immediately, the third man scrambled across the seat, opened the door, and fell onto the gravel.

I called for you to watch, but you were busy sending a telegraph. The scene happened repeatedly, perhaps four or five times. The men would thrust the man into the car, and, before they could stop him, he'd crawl across the seat and pitch himself out onto the driveway. His clothes had turned nearly white from the gravel dust.

Finally, the men wrestled their companion into the front seat, and one held him while the driver sprinted around the car and jumped in behind the wheel, blocking the errant man's exit. I heard the engine start, and the car sped away from the pumps and out of view. All that remained was a thin white cloud of gravel dust. Then I was alone again with my white, green, pink, and yellow forms, and I never did learn who those men were and what that strange drama was all about.

Now I sat on the other side of that window, pausing on my way out of town. I looked through the window, past the old desk and typewriter. You were a silhouette through the dirty screen, standing, hat still on, reading something in your hand. It was probably another freight bill from that endless stream that you dealt with every day.

I sat in my Plymouth for a moment or two and thought about dashing in for a final, quick visit. But we had said our farewells, or had tried to, and I didn't think I could do it again. So I let out the clutch and pulled away from the depot. In a moment, I passed the grade-school building on West Elm and those old white frame houses that lined the unchanging street where even the weeds beside the pavement seemed always the same.

At the end of West Elm, I angled onto the highway that led to Mt. Vernon, on to Joplin, and then into Oklahoma, where I'd find the route that would take me to Texas.

Soon, I could no longer see Republic's water tower in my rear view mirror. And by the time the Springfield radio stations had faded from my radio, I began to think more about what lay ahead than what I was leaving behind.

I didn't know, as I drove those last few miles of Missouri highway, that I would never see you again. I didn't know that I would never be able to tell you a proper goodbye. So, let this be it.

Don

Dear Jud:

One of my favorite recollections of our early years on East Elm Street is of standing on the rear floorboard of our Dodge sedan and, looking out the side window, watching the familiar panorama of Elm Street pass before my eyes at a leisurely, even stately, pace. But on one of those mornings, images of houses, trees, and sidewalks sped through my view at a speed that thrilled me and terrified Isabel. That was the day Isabel couldn't get the Old Dodge to go home.

I suspect it was Isabel who first began to call that car "the Old Dodge." In the one photo of it I recall seeing, it appeared to be a 1934 or 1935 four-door sedan. The incident I recall happened in 1939. You usually drove it to the depot unless Isabel needed to run errands, in which case you walked to work. On this particular day, Bob and I had accompanied Isabel to town for a visit to Lee Evans' grocery store. It was Evans Grocery's turn in Isabel's shopping cycle. There were three grocery stores on Main Street, and she patronized them in rotation. Fair habits like that don't go unnoticed in small towns.

After she'd made her grocery purchases, we stopped at the depot to see what time you'd be coming home that evening. Then Bob and I clambered into the back of the Old Dodge and Isabel set out for home. She made the left turn onto Elm Street at the library, and I could feel the tires bumping over rough places in the road as I stood on the floorboard of the car. I would usually stand on the right side and Bob would take the left side. At these stations, we would watch Elm Street's houses glide by.

Usually, as we approached the Haynes House—the name we used to identify our first home on Elm Street, a house you rented from a landlord named Haynes—the Old Dodge began to slow in front of the Renshaws', Isabel applied the brakes in front of the Mitchells', and I'd brace myself for the bouncy turn into our rutted driveway. That didn't happen on this day. Instead of slowing and turning into the driveway as we always did, we sailed right by our house. This puzzled me because, as we were leaving you, Isabel had said we were driving straight home. The front porch of our house receded from view, and I turned to look at Isabel. She was struggling with the controls. "Boys! Sit down!" she commanded. "The gas pedal's stuck and I can't get this thing to slow down!"

The last house on Elm Street was behind us now, and we were speeding over the gravel of Elm Street Road into the countryside east of Republic. The Old Dodge was leaving a large cloud of dust behind us. Isabel was muttering as she held the brake pedal down, trying to slow us. The Old Dodge didn't like that and began to buck furiously as we slowed. Isabel pressed the clutch pedal in and the engine, suddenly unrestrained, raced at a dangerous-sounding level. She let the clutch pedal out, the car lurched forward, and we were off again, gathering speed.

Somehow, Isabel brought the Old Dodge partially under control by the time we reached Stovers' Corner, and it seemed somewhat tamed as she turned into the Stovers' driveway. Whatever had made the Old Dodge run wild apparently had released its power. One of the Stovers peered at us from a window, probably wondering who the visitors were. Isabel backed our car out of the driveway, turned it around, and headed west for another try at our own driveway. This time, everything appeared to be normal.

Driving toward Republic, Isabel—unlike Mr. Stover—drove the Old Dodge in the proper gear. When Mr. Stover drove his car to Republic, he never shifted the transmission past second gear. You could hear his engine screaming a couple miles out as he sped toward town in at least one gear too low.

We began our trip back to town at a normal pace. Then I noticed that the car was picking up speed and I heard Isabel say, "Oh, no!" Again, we roared past our house and on down Elm

Street toward the business district. I watched the Cantrells' house flash by, and then the Eagans', Doc O'Dell's, and the Owens'. At that point, Isabel turned off the ignition to let the car coast past the lumberyard, braking it to a stop just before we reached Main Street. Isabel then turned on the ignition again, started the engine and cautiously shifted to low gear. As she turned the Old Dodge around, she said "We're going to go slow, boys, and if it acts up this time I'll turn the key off and we'll just walk home." We crept along Elm Street until she finally maneuvered the balky car into the driveway and stopped the engine. We were home at last.

At supper that night, Isabel described the Old Dodge's behavior. Years later, when we had a better understanding of mechanical concepts, you told us that you had taken the Old Dodge to Arrington Motors for a checkup but that their analysis had been inconclusive. You said they had examined the linkage to the accelerator and that it had seemed to be functioning properly. But they had recommended replacing it, just to play it safe, and that seemed to help. It must have, because I don't recall taking any more runaway rides in the Old Dodge.

That vehicle is prominent among my first memories associated with you. There are other, earlier memory fragments, but they're just flashes, brief and undefined as heat lightning. In one recollection, I can see your face inside the car and you aren't smiling. I'd strayed away from home in my pajamas, hoping to visit you at the depot. But the phone call from Isabel brought you out looking for me. Halfway to town on the sidewalk, I saw the Old Dodge coming toward me. You rolled to a stop, and when I climbed into the front seat, you told me sternly that I had done a very dangerous thing, and that I was never to do that again.

I believe there was something frightfully wrong with the Old Dodge. Not mechanically, but spiritually, perhaps. I don't truly believe that automobiles have spirits. But I have, at times, wondered whether the Old Dodge was haunted; made mean-spirited by a spiteful ghost, the remnant of some unhappy event that had occurred long before you bought the vehicle.

The doors, for example, sometimes closed at times that were, well, inappropriate. A rear door slammed shut while Bob's hand still gripped the door post, causing his fingers to swell up like little sausages. Another time, a door closed while I was still exiting the car, leaving a painful bruise on my ankle.

Doors opened mysteriously, too. There was a frightening incident near the end of a long, looping drive down blacktops and dusty back roads that took us first to a rickety farmhouse near Clever, then on to visit friends in Billings, then back to Republic.

On the first leg of our trip, Isabel drove down a dusty country road until we reached an old two-story house on some farmland outside Clever. The house had been painted at one time, but that was long ago, and most of the paint had been blasted away by years of sunlight, wind, and rain. The two elderly sisters who lived there were known for the quality of their quilt making, which was the reason for our visit. While Isabel gave them the specifications for the quilt she wanted, Bob and I explored their house. There was little to see downstairs, so we clumped up the steep wooden steps to the second floor, where we found only two dim, plain-walled bedrooms. There was a brittle, old smell about the house, like dried eggshells. The two old women seemed brittle and frail, too.

Isabel thanked the sisters and shepherded us back to the car. As we drove away, I stared out the back window and saw the lonely looking women waving to us from their front porch. They stayed on the porch, waving goodbye until they became tiny figures that faded into the pale beige dust from the gravel road.

Our next stop was in Billings, and after our visit there, we began the return trip to Republic. Isabel was driving slowly on the old blacktop road, and Bob and I each stood by a rear door, watching the countryside unroll outside our windows. On this return leg of our journey, we had switched our usual positions so that he was on the right side and I was on the left.

Without warning, Bob's door popped open and he tumbled out of the car and onto the shoulder of the highway. While Isabel was braking to a stop, I leaned over to watch Bob roll like a log through the weeds and down into a ditch. She leaped from the car and ran down into the ditch to retrieve Bob, who was squalling loudly. Luckily, his fall from the slow-moving Dodge had left him with just bruises and scratches. But after that episode, we were never again allowed to stand beside our doors.

We never determined what made the door spring open that way, just as Arrington Motors never divined the cause of the sticky accelerator that gave Isabel such a turn. My belief concerning the Old Dodge is that it had been owned by a gangster, probably in Chicago, before you bought it. He must have done something to enrage some rival gangsters who, probably using piano wire, surprised and garroted him while he was behind the wheel of the car. His spirit thus was doomed to ride forever in the Old Dodge, and when you became the owner, it began to go riding with us. That's just my theory.

But having a spirit in residence didn't give our car eternal life. I believe you would recall how it met its end.

On the morning of the day the Old Dodge died (or, more accurately, was murdered) Bob, Larry French, and I were playing a mindless game, as five-year-old boys often do. Larry had been allowed to come to our house to play, and when he arrived, Bob and I were eating our favorite treat: a sorghum sandwich. He stared hungrily at our sandwiches and said, "Wisht I had a sorghum sammich." We took him inside to see if Isabel would oblige. She smiled and laid two slices of white bread on the counter, spread a thick layer of butter on one, poured dark sorghum molasses on that, and covered it with the other bread slice. Presto! A sorghum sandwich. (I make them that way today—still messy and still delicious.)

We returned with our "sammiches" to the front yard, and soon we were dipping muddy water from a puddle in the driveway, pouring the water into a Folgers Coffee can, and then pouring it back into the puddle. I don't recall the objective of this effort, but it must have been a recycling operation of some sort.

We were still at it near noon when you arrived in the Old Dodge, home for lunch. We stood aside as you drove into the driveway, splashed through our puddle, and rolled to a halt. After you greeted us and went inside, we continued our game.

But now, a new element had changed the character of our game. It was the Old Dodge. There it sat, parked near our puddle. And the man who had left his car there wanted it filled with gasoline. Bob and I loved riding with you when you drove our car to the gasoline pump that sat in front of Owen and Short's hardware store. The pump looked so tall, with those cylindrical glass bowls on top full of orange-hued gasoline. Fred Short came out of the hardware store to hand-pump the gasoline by moving a long lever back and forth until the requested number of gallons had been transferred to the Old Dodge's gas tank.

So, while you were having lunch, we unscrewed the Old Dodge's gas cap, dipped the Folgers can into the puddle and filled the tank with liquid from our filling station's muddy pump.

We had finished refueling your car by the time you came out to drive back to the depot, and we stood watching as you climbed into the car. You pushed the starter and the engine started, then coughed, then quit. You tried again, and the engine again caught, then quit. For good. As much as you pressed the starter button, the engine would not ignite. The filling station men had brought to an end the era of the Old Dodge.

We watched the wrecker from Arrington Motors come to tow the Old Dodge away. It was an interesting operation, the way they put a big hook under the back of our car and then hoisted the rear wheels up into the air. I looked at the front of the car as the wrecker pulled it out of the drive and down Elm Street. The big, round headlights stared blankly toward the pavement.

You eventually learned what had happened to the Old Dodge's fuel system, and we were confined to quarters for an appropriate time. When I recall that incident now, I can still see the grille and the big, round headlight eyes of the Old Dodge receding from us down Elm Street. And I still wonder if it was my own remorse or the sad spirit that inhabited it that made the Old Dodge look so forlorn.

Don

The Firefly

The Firefly

Dear Jud:

I could tell by your face that you had important news when you came home from the depot that summer evening in 1943. As soon as you saw Bob and me, you said you had a big announcement, so hurry and get washed up. We did, and when we sat down to your favorite supper of fried round steak, mashed potatoes and gravy, and rhubarb pie for dessert, you made your announcement. You told us that in just a few days, the St. Louis–San Francisco Railway (which you always referred to simply as "Frisco") would be sending a new type of train through Republic. The train would arrive in the evening, when we wouldn't be in school, so we could all go watch it together.

You called this train a "streamliner," and said it was not only Frisco's first streamliner, it was one of only a few streamliners in America. You sounded proud when you told us the name of this streamliner: the Firefly.

I knew about fireflies. They were gentle, harmless little bugs that Bob and I chased all over the front yard on warm summer nights. They flashed their beacons for us, creating little golden pulses of light, first here, and then there, and then over there. We called them lightning bugs, and we had to be quick as lightning to catch one, snatching it from the air while its belly was still shining. Otherwise, it was impossible to catch them. We knew the night air was full of them, but they were invisible until they blinked their lightning, signaling their positions to potential mates. If one of us actually captured one of the creatures, we cupped it in two hands and studied the slender little flying beetle in the weak glow of its own light.

On a good night, we caught enough of the bugs to put them in a glass jar, which then became a magic lantern to show to you and

Isabel on the porch. We had to be careful with them, because they were so fragile that rough handling could make them come apart. Although I feel differently now, it didn't seem cruel then to mash off the soft, glowing section of the lightning bug's body, paste it on my finger and wear it like the phosphorescent gemstone of a ring.

So, after your announcement, I considered the name, "Firefly" in the context of what I knew about them. It didn't make sense for the Frisco to use this name for a fast, roaring, steam-powered streamliner.

I tried to visualize what the Firefly, the train, would look like. My mind created a vague, fantastic image of a huge insect-like machine, long and dark with bug-eye protuberances at the front, and orange-striped wing-like features folded along the top of the engine.

Later that evening, lying in bed on the back porch, which you and Isabel had screened in and converted into a bedroom for Bob and me since the other bedroom of our two-bedroom house belonged to our sisters, I thought about the Firefly as it might appear on its run through Republic. I saw the insect machine rushing along the tracks, coming toward the depot from the direction of Springfield, its impassive bug-face showing no feeling as it towed its long string of passenger cars.

The distant sound of a steam whistle started a travelogue in my mind as it always did. I saw coaches and Pullman cars gliding through the night. Inside the cozy, lighted cars, passengers sat, relaxing, reading, and snoozing. I switched the travelogue to another scene in which Bob and I were tucked into two Pullman berths. Then, magically, Bob and I appeared in the dining car at a table with a white tablecloth. A friendly waiter served a delicious dinner, which we ate while speeding through the night. We usually also visited the observation car, where men sat in upholstered easy chairs, drinking whisky and smoking cigars.

If the trains were heading east through Republic, I saw people getting off at Springfield's handsome train station with the white stucco walls and red tile roof, or perhaps at the cavernous (in my mind) Union Station in St. Louis. If the trains went west, the passengers were headed for Tulsa, probably, or even Texas—and I couldn't imagine what train stations looked like there.

In the dark, I clucked my tongue, imitating the rhythmic click-click, click-click … click-click, click-click … of the steel wheels passing over the rail joints. I remembered the "SL-SF" abbreviation for St. Louis–San Francisco Railway that I'd seen stenciled on box cars, and I discovered that substituting the SL-SF sound for the click-click sound was another way to imitate the sound of train wheels rolling over tracks: SL-SF, SL-SF … SL-SF, SL-SF … SL-SF, SL-SF … and soon I would drift off to sleep.

You knew the name of every passenger train that passed through Republic. In the evening, when you were in your green chair in the living room, the faint and lonely whistle of an approaching train would cause you to pull out your Frisco pocket watch and say, "That's the Will Rogers, right on time." You knew the other trains, too, and I loved the sound of their names: the Bluebonnet, the Meteor, the Texan, the Texas Special, the Oklahoma Special, and the Oklahoman.

Until you explained the naming protocol when we were older, Bob and I thought that the Frisco gave those names to the great locomotives that pulled the cars. We didn't understand that the names were marketing devices that the Frisco and other railroads used to promote their passenger services. And you knew not to try to explain that the locomotives were just the machines that made the passenger services possible.

None of those Frisco passenger trains actually served Republic, which was just a quick-passing patch of light to the passengers in the coaches. When I asked, once, why the depot's waiting room was always empty, you said that Republic was too close to Springfield for the engineers to bother stopping. You said we were so close to Springfield, in fact, that if they tried to let someone off at your depot, the passenger car might be in Republic but the engine would be in Springfield. So, they figured they might as well skip Republic and go on into Springfield. I knew that you were joking, but it helped me watch, unperturbed, as the trains roared through town at more than fifty miles an hour.

Isabel said that it would take an act of war to get Frisco to stop a passenger train in Republic, and as was so often the case, she was right.

During World War II, you'd let us stand by you in the doorway of the depot and watch as trains rushed through town pulling flatcars loaded with olive-drab tanks and jeeps, menacing-looking howitzers and anti-aircraft cannons, and other army materiel. And long troop trains clattered by, sometimes one or two each week, full of GIs staring at us through the windows. Most of the GIs waved back when we waved, but I was disappointed when one soldier stood on the observation platform of the last car of the train, grinning at me as he held up five fingers. As the car receded, he peeled down three fingers, banana fashion, leaving the middle one extended. I asked you what that meant, and you said he was just "shooting the finger." I asked you what that meant, and you said, "Oh, it's just a rude gesture. It's sort of an insult." I didn't understand why a GI would want to insult me. You explained that he was probably nervous about where he was going and would rather be my age, standing by a depot.

After the war finally ended, if I was at the depot at the right time, I saw passenger trains packed with soldiers speeding through town. On these trains, the soldiers in the windows seemed more relaxed, even bored-looking. And one morning, you said that one of these Frisco trains was actually going to stop at the depot to bring home from the war a man we knew as Li'l Abner.

We were close enough to the tracks to feel the heat of the locomotive as it rolled by us, slowing, the big drive wheels clanking and the steam engine chugging and thrumming. There was a loud metallic shriek and the first passenger train to stop in Republic in years came to a halt. A conductor stepped from the coach car in front of us and placed a stool beneath the steps. He gave a small salute as a tall man, looking fit and sharp in his uniform, emerged and stepped onto the gravel. I recognized Li'l Abner, who was grinning at the family members who had come to welcome him home. They kissed and hugged, and then they all turned and walked toward Main Street as steel wheels screeched and couplings clumped and the passenger train began to move again.

Sometimes, I wondered if it bothered you that only freight trains stopped in Republic, to leave or hook onto boxcars on the siding. The engineers who looked from the cabs of the speeding passenger locomotives sometimes gave you hardly any notice when you stood at the front of the depot. And when they approached the crossing at Main Street, near the depot, they blew the whistle in the same pattern that they used for all the other crossings in town: lonng, lonng, short, short, lonnnnng. I thought they should have devised a special whistle greeting for you.

Still, it was thrilling to stand in the depot doorway with you, only feet from the rails, braced against the superheated blast from a passing locomotive and feeling the ground tremble underfoot. I had to look through squinted eyes to watch the blurred image of the powerful steam pistons pushing the big rods that turned the huge drive wheels because the torrent of hot, oily-smelling air threw dust and cinders against my face.

Before the arrival of the Firefly, the Frisco railroad had done some cosmetic work on several locomotives to produce a streamlining effect. We got rare glimpses of one of these engines, pulling a Bluebonnet train, or it may have been the Texas Special. The cowcatcher had been smoothed, and curving up from it a sleek, white-painted band ran the length of both the engine and the coal car.

I often drew pictures of Frisco locomotives, and I began to draw them all with this white band and the Frisco name emblazoned inside the band. Beneath one of my sketches, I wrote the word "STREAMLINER," and I was struck by how much the word, printed in block letters, suggested the sleek, fast trains to which it referred.

After you announced the coming of the Firefly at supper that evening, I sat down with my drawing pad and tried to draw a picture of it. My first effort looked pretty much like the other streamliners I'd sketched. And try as I might, I found that I couldn't draw anything that suggested what the new streamliner might look like. Confusing images of bug-like engines kept coming to mind, and they were too difficult to render.

But I knew that I wouldn't be kept in suspense long, because I was going to see the real Firefly in only a couple of days. During your supper announcement, you explained, mostly to Isabel, that the new streamliner actually had made its inaugural run somewhat more than a year earlier and it had been in service between Kansas City and Oklahoma City. That route hadn't brought it through Republic or Springfield, but now it was making a special run that would.

Over the next two days, time seemed almost suspended, but the hour did come and we found ourselves walking with you and Isabel on our way to actually see the mysterious Firefly. I always enjoyed walking along Elm Street, which could be almost tunnel-like under the spreading branches of the elm trees, ash trees, and tall sycamores, but that evening, everything seemed to glow magically in the soft light.

We first walked to the depot, and then you decided that we should stand on Main Street, a safe distance from the tracks. At that distance and angle, you said, we should have a longer and better look at the Firefly. In my mind, I had seen the train coming toward us from the east, but you told us to look west toward Billings, since the Firefly was coming from Oklahoma, bound for St. Louis.

Bob and I fidgeted and ran up and down the rise that Main Street took to cross over the tracks. But we stood still when you checked your watch and said it was time for us all to look westward. A moment later, we heard a train whistle in the distance. I saw a small, dark shape headed our way. The dark shape grew larger at a surprising rate, quickly reaching the point where the tracks curved toward the depot, and I began to make out features of the thing that was racing toward us. The bug-like image I had anticipated disappeared as the real Firefly materialized a hundred yards away, closing that distance at a breathtaking rate.

It was like nothing I had expected. The aerodynamic shape of the Firefly's locomotive added to the sensation of speed as the streamliner rushed through the evening air like a bullet. And that is what this machine looked like to me: a long, bluish-gray projectile sweeping gracefully and almost soundlessly over the rails. And then it was upon us.

The top of the engine was as smooth as a torpedo; the smoke stack and the dome-like protrusions I was accustomed to seeing on locomotives were missing. Even the familiar, heavy plume of dark coal smoke was gone. Only shimmering heat waves issued from the low, wedge-shaped cowling above the nose (I learned later that the Firefly's boilers were fueled by oil, not coal). The headlight was recessed into the bullet-nose and a wide silvery stripe swept up from the cowcatcher, continuing not only along the side of the engine but along the sides of the oil tender and three passenger cars as well. As the Firefly thundered by directly in front of us, I glimpsed the blur of the huge driver wheels and the words "FRISCO LINES" stenciled on the silvery stripe above them.

I felt the noise and the heat of the steam engine and inhaled the familiar scorched oil and steam smell that always emanated from locomotives. And then I finally saw something insect-like: two huge eyes, which became the round windows on the rear of the lounge car of the now-rapidly receding train.

In a matter of seconds the Firefly was gone. There was nothing left but hot little whirlwinds in the wake of the Firefly's passing. I couldn't think of words to use for what I had just seen, and in that stillness, I realized that I was still holding my breath. Someone whistled, and you said something like "Wow!" and Isabel said, "Well, the Frisco's really got themselves something this time."

You stood quietly, looking eastward toward the dusk in which the Firefly had disappeared. I saw that your eyes were watery, and when you noticed my stare, you turned away and said you had a cinder in your eye.

On our walk home, you told us that there had probably never been a streamliner like the Firefly—anywhere. And then we all compared reactions to the sight of the Frisco's sensational new train. I was anxious to get home, because now I knew how to draw the Firefly. It was the most beautiful train I had ever seen, and I was so relieved that it looked nothing at all like a lightning bug.

Don

Dear Jud:

The thing that people need to know about those of us who happen to be twins is that we aren't necessarily two of a kind. Bob and I were always called twins, and all that that implies. But in fact, we were just brothers—fraternal twins—two individuals who were born ten minutes apart on the same day.

My own experience with being a twin has left me unable to see the symmetry in it that others may see. Bob and I were anything but a matched set. We couldn't have been more unlike if he were an Inuit and I were a Frenchman.

I have always wondered how Bob managed to be born first. You'd think that I'd have had a fifty-fifty chance of being Number One, but no. Bob must have elbowed me aside to go to the front of the line. And that set the pattern for the years to follow. He was the leader and I was the follower—a shadow and, on at least one occasion, an echo.

In school, Bob always excelled at math while I struggled with it. As I write this letter more than half a century later, I can easily summon back the anguish of those long nights at the card table, trying to grasp principles of arithmetic. You sat patiently with me, puffing your pipe, as you endeavored to help me solve those maddening "word problems" in my arithmetic book ("If Train A left Kansas City heading east at 50 mph and Train B left St. Louis heading west at 40 mph …") while my mind wandered off to other subjects, such as imagining how bad the wreck would be when Train A ran into Train B.

Bob always found it easy to talk to girls. But I could not imagine what to say to them beyond a sentence or two about fighter planes. He was a talented singer and loved to perform before an audience, while I cowered at the mere thought of it. I could carry a tune as well as he, but no one knew. I simply could not stand and sing for other people. The sound of my voice made me feel too vulnerable.

My deficiency in the performing arts appeared early. Miss Hadlock asked her second-grade class members to stand and sing a line from some simple little song. I believe it began, "I come from Montana, I wear a bandana ..." When it was my turn to sing, my face felt hot as I mumbled the words, feeling the eyes of all my class members boring into me. Miss Hadlock later told my sister Jean that she didn't think I could hear or carry a tune, and that I was "a monotone."

In the third grade, Mrs. Robertson organized a rhythm band. Once she had it fully energized, it sounded like one of those funeral processions you see in documentaries about China. It was a wonder, the way she forged that collection of gongs, cymbals, triangles, tambourines, wooden blocks, and sticks into a highly disciplined musical ensemble. She waved her baton at the noisy crowd and got us rolling, building momentum until we gradually began to clatter in a semblance of rhythm.

When I auditioned for the band, I tried out for triangle—the premier rhythm band instrument. But I wasn't chosen, Mrs. Robertson told Isabel, because I performed indifferently and seemed to be thinking about something else. I was given two wooden blocks and assigned to the back row of the band with the other malfeasants.

You couldn't have imagined how I hated being referred to as "shy." People kept saying, "Don's such a shy boy." Or "Isn't that Bobby a cutter? Not shy like his twin brother." I accepted that judgment because it was pronounced by adults—people who knew about such things.

One of the features of the PTA open house at Republic Grade School in the winter of 1944 was a play about a medieval king and his court. Bob, of course, won the lead role as the king. It was a meaty part, with paragraphs of dialogue to memorize. He easily mastered the lines and was ready to perform when the tattered velveteen curtains were jerked apart by giggling stage hands.

The tiny stage was on the north side of the big room on the second story of the grade school building, where both the seventh and eighth grades were taught. It was a cold Missouri night outside, but it was warm and close in the classroom as I awaited my cue.

Being shy, I had sought and was given a minor part as a page. The part required me to make one walk-on appearance, and I had but one line of dialogue to memorize. I remember it vividly, still:

"Your Majesty, a coach and four are just without the chamber door."

I had worked diligently on that line, repeating it over and over again, alone, in the basement, on the attic stairs, in the back yard, in trees—wherever I could practice without being heard. I was determined not to forget my line and to show you and Isabel that I could perform adequately, after all.

The play proceeded, and I stood out of sight on the edge of the little stage, still silently repeating my line. Bob was issuing royal commands to various members of his court, and soon Mrs. Land tapped me on the shoulder. It was my cue to walk onto the stage. As I did, my face flushed and I immediately forgot her instructions to turn partially toward the audience when I spoke my line. Anyway, I didn't want to face all those eyes that were watching my every move.

I slouched toward King Bob in my shabby page costume and, after bowing, I hurriedly mumbled my message:

"Yer Majisty a coach 'n four are jist without the chamber door."

Then I turned, not looking directly at the audience, but getting a glimpse of your face and Isabel's, and shambled off the stage. My drama career was over. I had delivered my one and only line without error—and without the slightest trace of inflection or emotion. I was a robot. But when you and Isabel came to the stage after the play, you praised me for remembering all the words and for pronouncing them so well.

That night, Isabel fixed hot cocoa to warm us before we climbed under the covers of our bed on the back porch. I huddled under the heavy blankets and relived my moment on stage. This time, the faces of parents watched with rapt attention as my voice rang out, forcefully, crisply, my Missouri twang transformed by just the trace of a British accent: "Your Majesty! A coach and four are just without the chamber door!"

I first heard Fred Lowery whistle during a radio variety show you were listening to. The show featured one of your favorite dance bands, Horace Heidt and His Musical Knights. Lowery was a featured performer with the band, and on this night he was whistling a piece called "Shepherd's Serenade." The clarity and beauty of that music stopped me in my tracks. I stood by your green easy chair, listening with you until he finished the piece. When you told me Fred Lowery was blind, you might have noticed that the news had great impact. I thought about what it must be like to live in perpetual darkness. And, thinking about these things for the first time, I marveled at what kind of person this Fred Lowery must have been to make music like this despite his blindness.

I was already a constant whistler, but I began to practice Lowery-like whistling when no one was around to hear me. I taught myself to whistle another of Lowery's hit tunes, "Deep in the Heart of Texas." Before long I was able to offer a reasonably good imitation of his lyrical technique, and I applied it to various popular tunes such as "I Love You Truly," and "So Tired," all ornamented with Lowery-esque vibrato and trills.

With more practice, I developed ornamentations of my own. I found that, by holding my lips and tongue in certain positions, I could produce two harmonizing notes at once. I taught myself a flutter-tonguing technique which I used to copy Elmo Tanner's rendition of "Heartaches." And as time went by, I began to fantasize that, given the chance, I could stand up and whistle on a par with the great ones.

In 1947, a notice in the window of Eagan's Market offered me that opportunity. The small poster announced that a candy company representative would conduct a talent contest at the grocery store and the grand prize was to be a silver dollar. Lesser prizes of ribbons and candy bars also would be awarded.

Bob and I had been practicing scales and simple tunes on the plastic "Tonette" flutes you and Isabel had given us some weeks earlier. Bob also had improvised some other tunes, including his version of the then-popular "My Heart Sings." We decided that we should enter the contest. I thought about my whistling, and I wondered if the upcoming contest would be the day my marvelous musical talent was to be revealed to the world. In my mind I could hear my own rendition of Fred Lowery's "Indian Love Call," and I fantasized about interviews and personal appearances on Springfield's radio stations, KWTO and KGBX.

On the morning of the talent show, Bob pocketed his Tonette and we walked to Eagan's Market. I left my Tonette at home. The candy representative was behind the check-out counter at the front of the grocery store when we arrived, and several people were listening to his explanation of the talent show rules, which were simple enough. Contestants would perform, and the winner would be determined by the amount of applause he or she received from the audience.

I looked around to see who else was planning to perform, and I wondered if I would have the nerve to step forward when it was time. Only a few classmates were in the small crowd, and I could tell by their smirks that they had no intention of entering the contest.

The candy man finished his remarks and asked for the first contestant. No one moved. People pointedly looked at each other to make it clear to the candy man that he shouldn't call on them. I thought again about whistling "Indian Love Call," or my harmonizing, two-tone version of "I Love You Truly," but the hot, clammy feeling was coming on and I kept still.

Bob finally held up his hand, and the candy man enthusiastically called him forward. I'm not sure if you had ever heard the song, "My Heart Sings," but the tune, basically, was a run up and down the musical scale. The song begins with the bottom note of the scale, climbs, note by note, to the top of the octave and then, with a simple variation, moves back down again.

After the grinning candy man announced the selection, Bob quickly launched into the song, blowing nice, clear notes on the Tonette. He began to work his way meticulously up the ladder of the tune. At this point, the candy man was beaming at Bob and the onlookers. But Bob, inspired by his moment in the spotlight, played relentlessly through the entire song, with variations, and then, anticipating an encore, played the entire thing again. At this point, the candy man had stopped beaming and was staring at Bob's Tonette with a wooden grin and a glassy look in his eyes.

Eventually, Bob played the last note and modestly took the Tonette from his mouth. The candy man quickly clapped his hands and, indicating that the crowd should join him, shouted, "Well, now, that was really something! Who wants to be next?"

I wanted to hold up my hand and wow the people with my whistling renditions, but I couldn't. Old Devil Shy had got me again.

No one else volunteered, either, so the candy man moved ahead. "Okay," he said. "Looks like we have a winner!" Here, he paused to build suspense before pointing at Bob. "And the winner is ... Bob Alderman! Step up here, Bob!" I joined in the applause and watched Bob receive his silver dollar and First Place ribbon.

That afternoon when I was alone in the basement— the acoustics were just right for whistling over by the fruit room—I whistled a medley of my best pieces. I warmed up with "I Love You Truly," adding a nice improvised chorus in which the warbles harmonized. I then breezed through "Heartaches" and a harmonizing two-tone version of "Indian Love Call," and finished with a dazzling, flutter-tonguing performance of "Flight of the Bumblebee." All of the performances were, I thought, quite good.

If only I had had the courage, I might have advanced the art of whistling, a lost musical form seldom heard on our radios today.

You might have told me that I hid my talent under a bushel. You could have added that I also hid it behind a bedroom door one uncomfortable afternoon.

You knew, of course, how much Isabel missed the social activities that were so important to her during your years in Ozark. She was prominent there, with her poetry writing and readings and her work with the clubs and guilds. Many years later, she gazed out of the window of her apartment and told me how different life was for her after you moved the family to Republic and how much she missed the literary activities that she had found so fulfilling in Ozark.

But she did join the women's organizations in Republic, and, in the time left after caring for Bob and me, she became a member of the Arts and Crafts Guild, the Ladies Aid Society, the Methodist Women's Auxiliary, the Eastern Star, and the Women's Christian Temperance Union. Those organizations and activities were important not only to her but to the sense of community they helped impart. In my time, and in our insular neighborhoods, that quality is too often missing.

Isabel occasionally hosted social meetings at our house, and I learned to dread those because Bob and I were made to take baths and dress like twins and stand appealingly while the ladies cooed and clucked at us. Isabel knew the limits of our model behavior, and I'm sure she was relieved when we took the first opportunity to disappear.

The Arts and Crafts Guild meetings usually began with a business session in which the members discussed individual and community arts projects. That was followed by refreshments and entertainment, and it was during this segment of the meetings that Isabel was sometimes asked to read her poems.

You were safely at the depot during the Arts and Crafts Guild meeting Isabel hosted in 1943, when Bob and I were in the fourth grade. She had decided not to read her poems at this meeting. Instead, she had decided to surprise the ladies with a musical treat provided by the twins. When we heard what she was planning, Bob was all for it. I wanted to die.

For our performance, Isabel had decided that we would sing "Little Sir Echo," a cutesy and popular tune that I had first heard on one of the Springfield radio stations. I didn't care for it. I envisioned it being sung by a darling, Shirley Temple–type of child star. In my mind, I pictured the brat tilting her curly head and cupping a pudgy hand at her ear to catch the "echo" part of the lyrics.

Isabel arranged and choreographed our tune, and we rehearsed it once or twice on the day before the meeting. Bob, with his clear, true voice, sang the melody. I got the "echo" part because Isabel knew that I would not sing and was generally unreliable in these situations. She feared, correctly, that I would stand mute and glassy-eyed before the ladies.

My echo chamber, therefore, was to be in the corner of your bedroom, since that room was adjacent to the living room, where the ladies would be. I liked that part, Jud, because when the door was opened and pushed as far as it would go against the bedroom corner wall, it created a cozy little hiding place. Isabel decided that I should stand in this hiding place and provide the echo as needed.

So, I stood there while we practiced our number. When Bob sang the lyrics, "Little Sir Echo, how do you do? Hello!" it was my job to reply with a soft "Hello!" as if from afar. It all went pretty well during our rehearsals on the day before the meeting.

I lived in dread for the next twenty-four hours. And by the time the ladies began to arrive, I was miserable—hating both the prospect of our upcoming number and the itchy, 100 percent wool cuffs of the knickers Isabel made us wear.

Bob and I stayed out of sight while the club members conducted their business. This part of the meeting dragged on and on but, after a time, I began to smell coffee percolating in the kitchen. This signaled that our moment of destiny was near. Isabel soon came to prepare us for our performance and to herd me into my hiding place. From there, I heard her announce that today the guild members were going to hear the twins sing "Little Sir Echo." The ladies applauded.

Even though I was concealed behind the bedroom door my face was hot with stage fright and embarrassment. And then I heard Bob's voice. "Little Sir Echo, how do you do? Hello!" he sang, brightly. "Hello," I mumbled, tunelessly.

I could hear Bob's voice ringing from the living room as he sang the precious lyrics. And each time he sang out "Hello," I murmured a hollow hello in response. The number seemed to go on forever, but I finally echoed the last hello and the ladies applauded vigorously. Although our performance was over, I stayed in my corner, listening to the babble of conversation and the clinking of cups and saucers and smelling the pleasant aroma of coffee. I waited, not wanting to reveal myself in my itchy knickers, until Isabel came and led me into the living room. Bob was already busy with coconut cake and punch. I heard someone say, "Oh, there's the little echo now."

The living room was warm and wonderfully fragrant with the mingled aromas of coffee, fresh pie and cake, and ladies' perfume. I joined Bob with my dessert and gradually began to feel less conspicuous.

One by one, the ladies of the Arts and Crafts Guild began to make their goodbyes. As the members departed, they thanked Isabel for the lovely program and told her how much they enjoyed our song.

At the front door, one of the guests—a woman Isabel didn't care for and had in the past referred to as "that old battle-ax"— turned and said to Bob and me, "I liked your song so much, boys." Then, she inclined her head toward me and said with a narrow-eyed smile, "But I could barely hear the echo." Glancing at Bob, she said, "Maybe if you sing louder next time, Bobby, Little Sir Echo will come back stronger, too."

I smiled back at her, but in my mind I was saying "Want to bet, you old battle-ax?" in the meanest tone I could imagine.

I didn't actually say that, of course. But if I had, I wonder if you and Isabel might have chuckled about it later.

Don

Dear Jud:

You wouldn't have known, when you walked by her house on your way to the depot, that Mrs. Hale was a witch.

She looked nothing like the grotesque crone in Walt Disney's *Snow White*, which we had seen earlier in that year of 1939. Just the opposite. As a young woman, she must have been very beautiful. Even as an elderly woman, her face was still favored by delicately formed features. Her skin was smooth, with only fine little lines where, on the faces of others her age, there'd have been deep wrinkles. She kept her hair pulled into a perfectly neat bun. And when she looked at Bob and me, we saw eyes that were intensely blue, curious, and kind.

Mrs. Hale revealed that she was a witch one morning while we were playing in the driveway at Kenneth Renshaw's house. She lived next to the Renshaws, who lived next to the Mitchells, who lived next to us when we lived in the rented house that we always referred to as "the Haynes House." You would have walked past her small house on your way to and from work, and I'm sure you must have spoken to her on occasion. But she apparently never raised the subject of her witchery, or I'm sure you would have mentioned it at supper.

She seemed to stay inside her house most of the time, appearing on her front porch now and then to water her potted plants. Sometimes, we saw her poking around in the tidy little flower garden on the east side of her house.

I miss the pleasant proximity of our Elm Street neighbors— the easy, comfortable intimacy of small town life. That morning, Mrs. Hale watched from her porch as we squatted in Kenneth's driveway, playing with our toy cars. She called to us and asked what we were doing. Although I can't recall our reply, it must have amused her because she continued watching us for some time before she went inside. Perhaps half an hour passed before she appeared again. She called us over to her porch this time. From the screen door behind her, I could smell the aroma of things cooking inside, and I wondered if she was about to invite us in for breakfast. I thought to myself that we would have to ask Isabel first.

"Would you boys like to see some magic?" she asked. Kenneth and I nodded yes, and Bob, of course, said that he wasn't sure she could do magic. She assured us that she could and stood with her hands on her hips, glancing around her small yard.

"Hmm, let me see now," she said. Then, spotting something, she said, "I know what I'll do." She pointed toward her small flower bed, and asked us each to bring her one of the smooth, rounded river stones she had used to line the edges of the flower bed. She instructed us to choose stones that were about the size of our fists.

The three of us knelt by the garden and, clenching our fists, compared them to the row of rocks. I selected one of the round, yellowish rocks and carefully lifted it from its resting place. Mrs. Hale held an old baking pan toward us and we placed our stones in it.

"Now, wait here just a little while," she said, "and I'll have a surprise that I think you're going to like." Then she went into her house.

We waited for a short time that seemed like a long time, and, pretty soon, Mrs. Hale returned to the front porch. She was holding the same flat baking pan, but when she bent and extended the pan toward us, we saw that it held three golden cupcakes approximately the size of the river stones we had given her. Little wisps of steam were still rising from the cupcakes, and I could smell their delicate, lemony fragrance.

"Here, take your stones back," she told us. "I changed them into cupcakes!" We each took one of the stone cakes. Because it formerly had been a rock, I bit tentatively into mine. But my teeth sank into it as if I were biting air. It was that tender and light, and the vanilla flavor, with just a hint of lemon, filled my mouth and nose. She watched us gulp down the cakes, and she smiled.

Bob asked her how she was able to turn rocks into cupcakes. That's when she said, "Because I'm a witch." She chuckled at the expression on our faces and told us that not all witches were bad. There were good witches, like her, who could do good magic. She smiled down at us from her porch and told us that if we visited her again someday, she might have another surprise for us.

When Mrs. Hale went inside, I walked over to investigate the rock border of her flower garden. Three empty spaces marked the spots where our treats had come from, and I noticed that there were stones there for many more cupcakes. To my five-year-old mind that row of stones was full of promise, and Mrs. Hale's powers were wonderful, indeed.

Bob and I returned to Mrs. Hale's house the following day. When she answered the door, we asked if we could bring her some more rocks. She said, "Oh, I'm sorry boys. My magic isn't very strong today. But if you'll come back on Saturday morning maybe it will be working again." I looked at her garden as we walked away, and I saw that the rock border was complete again. She must have used her magic to grow new stones where the others had been.

On Saturday morning, we were back, and this time she allowed us to bring her two stones from the border. Then she said to bring her two more, because the magic felt extra-strong this morning. She took the four stones inside and in a short time returned with four golden stone cakes—two for each of us. We sat on the edge of her porch to eat the cakes, and they were as light and lemony and delicious as the first ones had been.

She watched us with those deep blue eyes as we finished off her gifts, and I remember thinking how lucky we were to have such a nice woman on our street—even if she was a witch. I had no notion then, of course, that our wondering acceptance of her magic was perhaps as pleasurable to her as the flavor of those delicious, golden sweets was to us.

Republic was a small place. But, I'm fairly certain that Mrs. Hale, good witch that she was, probably did not know Mr. Peavey, odd and mysterious as he was. Mr. Peavey didn't speak and didn't work anywhere that I could see. He just appeared on the streets and then disappeared. I asked you once where he lived and who he lived with. You said you weren't certain; somewhere on North Main Street, maybe, or was it over by Buddy Simpson's, behind the canning factory?

Mr. Peavey was a small man, probably no more than five feet tall. Although he seemed older to me when I was an adolescent, he probably was no more than forty-ish. He wore a pinch-bill cap, always, and an old raincoat, rain or shine, summer and winter. He used the coat's deep pockets to carry the things he found during his wanderings.

You mentioned that you saw him sometimes wandering along the main line tracks toward Billings, and you worried that he might not hear a train coming until it was too late. I saw him occasionally walking beside the spur tracks that lay between the cold storage building and the millpond. I saw him most often downtown, walking at the edge of the sidewalks of the two-block business district, bent slightly and staring at the pavement along the curbs. I believe he searched primarily for money, the small change that fell from the doors of parked cars or from pedestrians' pockets. But I also saw him pick up bottle caps, empty bottles, broken combs, cigar and cigarette butts, and tinfoil from cigarette packages.

I learned that it did no good to speak to Mr. Peavey if I happened to encounter him on the streets. He never replied. He just looked at me with an astonished expression, as if I had told him that I had just seen Hitler.

He did try to communicate something to me once. I saw him standing in the street in front of O'Dell's Drug Store, and, as I approached, he reached into his coat pocket and pulled out an object. I paused, and when he extended his hand toward me, I saw that he was holding a dead sparrow. I looked at him, and he gave me what may have been a questioning look. I couldn't tell. The look might have meant, "Would you like to have this dead bird?" More likely, it was "Would you like to *buy* this dead bird?" But I wasn't sure, so I just nodded amiably and said something like, "Um hmm!" He stared at me for a moment, I think trying to comprehend *my* meaning. Then he seemed to tire of dealing with me; he shoved the sparrow back into his pocket and shuffled off down the street.

I haven't thought of Mr. Peavey in years. But now I'm wondering if he might simply have been offering to share a valued possession with me. Perhaps he was even lonelier than he looked and saw something in my face that stirred a need to have an exchange of some sort with another human. But I wouldn't have learned anything more about that, because for the few years that I continued to see him inspecting the streets and gutters, he never again glanced back at me or acknowledged in any way that I was present.

Jud, if I were able, I might say to you, just for effect, "How about Danny Prater?" I believe I'm correct in thinking there were things about Danny that made you uneasy. He was in the eighth grade when Bob and I were in the sixth grade, and he was probably even older than that suggests. But that wasn't all of it, I suspect. What you probably found more unsettling was a certain earthy quality about Danny, the restless, knowing look in his eyes. You may have feared he would tell us things about girls that we didn't need to know yet. You probably smelled cigarette smoke on his clothes. And, in your view, anyone as worldly as Danny appeared to be might introduce us to other evils, such as whiskey and beer. If you had asked me outright, I could have told you that you needn't have worried.

Danny lived with his mother east of Republic, not too far from Highway 60. I used to wonder about his father, who never seemed to be around—and I don't recall that Danny ever mentioned him.

Maybe not having a father around was one reason Danny was so resourceful. He just knew how to do things.

He knew how to smoke, for instance, and he did it with his mother's permission. She kept a pack of Camels and a Zippo lighter on their kitchen table, and when Danny wanted a smoke, he'd say, "Hey, Ma, how 'bout a cig?" And she would say, without looking up from her reading or sewing, "Sure, help yourself." Her easy, casual acquiescence always amazed me; it was so unlike the reaction we would have expected from you or Isabel.

Danny was an ideal companion on long winter walks in the fields and woods east of town. When we came to one of the barbed wire fences that sectioned the fields, Danny put a hand on a fence post and sprang over, tucking his legs to clear the top wire. We had to push the top strand of barbed wire down and climb over, gingerly, a leg at a time, taking care not to catch our crotches on one of the barbs.

If we spotted a rabbit in a field, Danny moved reflexively, swooping to grab a rock and fire it at the rabbit all in one motion. And he could sail a rock so close to a buzzard on a dead tree branch, you could almost hear the bird cry "Whoa!" before it rose on its great wings and flapped away.

I loved to walk through the rows of a cornfield and feel the rough edges of the leathery leaves scraping at my jacket. The cold air sharpened the tobacco-like smell of the corn plants, which had given up their ears and were waiting out their days. Danny showed us how to rip a corn stalk out of the ground, knock clods of dirt off the end and hurl the plant like a spear. He could throw a corn stalk fifteen or twenty yards.

Danny also knew how to smoke bees away from their honeycombs and steal the dark, wild honey. We rode our bikes with him to Wells Pond north of Republic one fall afternoon so that he could show us the wild honey tree he had discovered. He said we needed to try some wild honey, because it was much better tasting than the tame honey from grocery stores.

Danny took us to the tree and pointed out a hollow in the trunk. There, he said, were the bees and their honey. I could see a few bees buzzing in and out of the large hole. Danny nodded, and we got out the empty jars we'd brought along for the honey raid.

He leaned his bike against the tree, climbed onto the frame and stood on the tattered seat. I handed him several pages of newspaper, which he rolled into a cylinder. He lit the end with a match, and, when the paper roll was blazing, he turned it upside down and dropped it into the hole in the tree trunk. He then leaped from his bike and we all ran to the other side of the pond to see what would happen.

Danny told us to get ready for a cold swim. "If them bees come this way, we're gonna get wet," he said. Smoke billowed from the bee hole, and soon a mass of angry bees came pouring out. They buzzed in a loose cloud briefly before rising up and away from the smoke. Danny yelled at us to bring the jars, and we followed him back to the tree. We watched as he climbed onto the bike seat and thrust his arm into the tree. When he pulled out his arm, he was holding a large, dark-brown mass. He jumped to the ground and, ignoring several groggy bees that were crawling on his sticky arm, he broke the honeycomb into chunks small enough to fit into our jars. We were filling the fourth jar when the bees returned and began to buzz at us, so we retreated to the pond again.

I stuck two fingers into one of the jars to try the wild honey, which was the color of motor oil. The flavor was musky and feral, like the creatures that had fed on wildflower nectar to make their honey. Danny said it tasted good, and I agreed because I thought that if I tried enough of this strange, wild honey, it would, in fact, begin to taste good.

It wasn't on this trip to Wells Pond, but on another, that Danny saved Bob from a dangerous snakebite. Danny had brought along a package of his mother's Camels, and he also had brought a couple of Hav-A-Sweet cigars for Bob and me. We sat on the bank of the pond, blowing smoke into the clear, wintry air. Bob sat cross-legged, leaning back with his arms against the sloping bank behind him.

Danny, who was beside Bob, suddenly said, very quietly, "Bob, don't move. Just don't move." Only a foot from Bob's arm, a snake that might have been a water moccasin was sluggishly coiling itself to strike at Bob. Danny moved with amazing speed, striking the snake sideways. The glancing blow uncoiled the reptile enough from him to grab its tail. Still on his knees, Danny swung the snake hard in an arc, smashing its head into the hard ground. That stunned the reptile, and Danny flattened its head with the heel of his boot.

We were enthusiastic in our praise for what he had done, but Danny said that he was used to doing that sort of thing. In fact, he said, he had a collection of skins from snakes he had killed, and some of them were rattlers. He invited us to his house to see a large rattlesnake skin that he was using to make a belt.

After school several days later, we rode to Danny's house to see his snake skins. There were only three rooms in the house. The kitchen and a seating area with a table and couch were in one room. A divider curtain hung from the ceiling, and behind it was Danny's bed. In another small room was his mother's bed and a doorway that revealed a tiny bathroom.

As we sat at the kitchen table admiring Danny's copperhead and rattlesnake skins, his mother announced that it was time for him to wash his hair. He protested, saying that he had company, but she said it would take only a minute or two, and that we could wait.

Danny walked to the kitchen sink and stuck his head under the faucet. Mrs. Prater used a bar of Ivory soap to work up a lather, and scrubbed his hair vigorously. Then came the rinsing, and the way it was done astounded us. As Mrs. Prater held Danny's head under the faucet to rinse away the lather, she reached into a box under the sink and gave him a white pad to hold over his eyes.

Bob and I looked at each other. We recognized the white object from magazine advertisements we had seen. Our friend Danny was shielding his eyes with a sanitary napkin!

You might wonder if that diminished Danny in our eyes. It didn't. He remained something of a hero to us. But as we grew older, we began to see less and less of him. Some years later, we heard that he had joined the army. I could see Danny at some army camp learning to be a soldier and impressing everyone with his marksmanship. The part I couldn't visualize was what he did when he had to share a shower room with the other men and it came time to rinse his hair.

Don

Dear Jud:

I was thinking about a couple of our family traditions recently, and thought I'd share them with you. Bob and I must have been six or seven years old—it was in that time just before Pearl Harbor—when Phyllis and Patty decided to establish a holiday tradition. Each evening during the week before Christmas, Bob and I were instructed to sit on the floor by the living room fireplace to drink cocoa and listen while our sisters took turns reading Charles Dickens's *A Christmas Carol* aloud. Jean, I'm sure, would have joined her sisters in this effort if she hadn't been away on her teaching job in Humansville. (That's one of the Missouri town names that always caused you to chuckle and shake your head.)

You seemed to enjoy those readings as you sat in the "Punish Chair," your green easy chair so named by Isabel because it was where Bob and I were so often banished to reflect upon our misdeeds.

I don't recall that we ever made it all the way through the novel in one of these week-long annual readings. But by skipping parts of the story that were too weighty for six- and seven-year-old minds, the girls managed to dramatize Ebenezer Scrooge's transformation from a mean-spirited grouch to a grateful and generous old man. At the end of the storytelling, however, I wasn't thinking about the lesson Scrooge had learned; I was thinking about the ghosts that came to haunt him.

And even today, when I think of those visitations in Ebenezer's gloomy chambers, I recall the tingling-yet-delicious dread that I associated with another holiday tradition: Christmas Day with the Moore family. At the time, you and Isabel might have assumed that what Bob and I liked best about this annual gathering was the holiday road trip to Ozark, where the Moores lived, or the wonderful food we'd be served. That was part of it, of course. But what we anticipated most happened after Christmas dinner, when we'd sit on the floor near Tom Moore and listen to one of his horrific ghost stories.

I was too young to really appreciate how valuable some friendships are, but I understood that there was something special about the Aldermans' relationship with Tom and Ethel Moore. You and Isabel had formed a bond with them during the years you were the Frisco agent in Ozark. And in 1933, when you moved twenty miles away to Republic, sustaining that friendship must have been very important to both you and the Moores. You kept the ties strong with frequent visits throughout the year, capped by a Christmas Day get-together, either in Ozark or Republic.

It never occurred to me to ask how a depot agent could become fast friends with a circuit judge who lived in a big house at the top of a hill in Ozark. I can't recall seeing Judge Tom dressed in anything but a dark business suit, with starched white shirt, tie, and vest. At first, I found his penetrating eyes and bushy, black eyebrows somewhat forbidding, but that appearance was contrary to his jolly, affable manner. When we spoke to Ethel Moore, it felt natural to call her "Mama Moore," which was the name she seemed to prefer. How easy it must have been to form the warm friendship you enjoyed.

The Moores and their daughters lived in an imposing, three-story brick home, and I especially liked the way the driveway at the side of their house was covered by a tall porte cochere. On the Christmas Day I'm about to recall, I stared at their house as you parked our car under their porte cochere. Bob and I had told our friends that the Moores lived in a mansion. In my mind, I compared it to our modest home. As I did, I asked you if we were poor. You said, "No, not poor. Just different."

As we clambered out of the car, I could smell the aroma of Mama Moore's Christmas dinner still cooking. After the door was closed on the cold air and bright sunlight, the interior of the house seemed dim. And an ominous feeling came over me when our sisters and the Moore girls took Bob and me aside to tell us about the crazy woman who lived in the attic. They led us to a landing on the second floor and pointed to a narrow stairway which led to the third floor. They warned us never to go up those stairs, knowing, of course, that we would disregard that advice at the first opportunity. Then they led us back down the stairs to the dining room, where the lights were bright and the smells of turkey, dressing, hot rolls, gravy, and coffee mingled.

The Christmas dinner was delicious, and I heard Isabel say that no one could make oyster dressing better that Mama Moore's. The older girls served dessert and coffee, and after Bob and I finished our dessert, we left the table to wander around. We wandered directly to the stairs and climbed to the second floor. The warm lights and familiar voices were below us, and we were alone. We walked down the hall to the small stairway that led to the third-floor chambers, and when I stared up into the gloom at the top of the stairs, the outline of a door was barely visible. I thought of the picture of the mad woman I had seen in Jean's copy of *Jane Eyre*, and, as I looked at the closed door above, I envisioned a wild-eyed, stringy haired hag, grinning cruelly as she waited for someone to open the door.

Bob had just placed a foot on the first step when we heard a soft "heh, heh, heh, heh." He brought his foot back quickly, and we looked at each other. "Heh, heh, heh," came the soft cackle again. I looked down the hallway but could see nothing except shadowy doorways. I felt a prickling in the small of my back as I turned and ran with Bob toward the main staircase. Neither of us noticed that one of the hallway doors closed slightly as we dashed by.

We reached the dining table downstairs just in time to see Tom push back his chair, dab his mouth with the linen napkin and say, "Well, now. Let's go into the library and talk." That meant it was time for one of his stories.

Isabel and Mama Moore decided to stay at the table for another cup of coffee, but the rest of us moved to the library for what we hoped would be another of Tom's hair-raisers. You and Tom sat in the two large leather wingback chairs, and we sat in a semi-circle on the carpet. My stomach tingled in anticipation as I watched you stoke your pipe and Tom clip the end of a huge cigar with a pair of scissors.

Recalling that moment, Jud, I think what a shame it is that entertainment technology in my time has displaced the storyteller; we're either too sophisticated or too self-conscious to indulge in this activity, with the result that storytelling may soon be a lost art.

But back to that Ozark Christmas. Tom put a lit match to the end of the cigar and puffed on it until a thundercloud of smoke hung over his head. He coughed, took the stogie out of his mouth, held it before him, and studied the smoldering end. The room was still as he looked somberly at each of us for a moment. Finally, he began the story in a hushed, husky voice.

"I knew this old-timer down near Harrison, Arkansas," he said, stopping to cough again and clear his throat heroically. All of Tom's stories began with "I knew this ..." He knew this old widow woman, and he knew this young man, and he knew this country preacher ...

Tom picked up the story. "He lived in a one-room cabin about twenty miles out of Harrison, and you had to travel five of those miles up a one-lane dirt road. It was a fur piece out in the country, it was—and completely isolated. Not too many people besides me knew this old-timer or where he lived. He lived alone, except for a single companion: his old bird dog named Drum.

"The old-timer and Drum lived in utter isolation. They were seen but once a month when they came by horse-drawn wagon into Harrison for provisions."

Tom paused, took several long drags on the cigar, and stared at the ceiling for a moment. Then he addressed the semi-circle again, gazing owlishly at each of as he resumed the story.

"One night there was a terrible lightning storm, like the one you had in Republic a while back. Remember?"

Bob and I nodded. I looked at you, and you smiled as you nodded along with us.

"Well, then, you know what it must have been like for that old-timer, alone in his little cabin down there in the Ozarks. The lightning was flashing," Tom waved his arms wildly in demonstration, "and the thunder was crashing and the wind was blowing rain so hard that it shook the old-timer's cabin!" Tom grabbed the sides of his leather chair and it creaked as he rocked it back and forth.

"But the old-timer was used to our Ozark storms, and he had a big fire in the fireplace, and Drum was lying beside him as he watched the flames dancing." We glanced at the fire in Tom's fireplace as he continued.

"Suddenly, there was a noise outside the cabin—a soft, strange sound. The old-timer, who was nodding off before the cozy fire, jerked his head up and listened." Tom demonstrated with his own head and sat motionless, eyes intent as if he, too, were listening for a sound. I looked uneasily toward the dark corner of the library.

"Old Drum raised his head up and perked his ears. He whimpered softly. Dogs can hear things humans can't, y'see. The old-timer and Drum sat as still as statues, listening." Tom raised one hand and held it in the air.

"They listened," he whispered, "listened, and heard the wind in the trees, and the thunder, and the rain beating down, and—wait! There it was again! A soft thump outside, something bumping against the door of the cabin out there in the woods, far from everything. Drum jumped to his feet and faced the door, hackles up, growling low in his throat. The old-timer hesitated, then got up. He stood listening, then walked carefully to the door.

"Cautiously, the old-timer lifted the iron latch and opened the door just a crack. Cold, wet wind blasted through the opening as the old-timer squinted into the darkness. He saw ..." Tom paused dramatically, "nothing. The storm was blowing outside as the old-timer eased the door open for a better look—and as he did," Tom's voice lowered ominously, "something soft and cold brushed against him—and came inside.

"Old Drum jumped back, cowering and barking hysterically. But after the old-timer slammed the door and clicked the latch down, he turned to face an empty room. He could see nothing except Drum, who had stopped barking and was crouched by the fireplace, quivering and whimpering.

"The old-timer went to the dog and bent down. 'Easy, old fellow, easy,' he said. But the dog just cowered against the cabin floor, shaking."

Tom leaned forward in his leather chair, eyes shining, face tense. "And then came a sound behind the old-timer, an awful, wet, thumping sound that froze his blood. He turned slowly around but still could see nothing in the room. But the sound was there, inside the cabin, against the wall. It came again, a moist, sucking thump—this time, higher on the wall. The old-timer stood frozen in the center of the cabin, too frightened to move. Thump! Again, that awful sound, higher still against the wall. It came again and again, thumping up the wall, across the ceiling and back down the opposite wall.

"Then, the sucking, thumping sound retraced its path, up that wall, across the ceiling and back down the other wall. The old-timer crouched on the floor, eyes bugging as he tried to follow the bumping, which was moving faster and faster up and across the inside of his cabin. Faster and faster went the horrible sound, and louder and louder, until the old-timer was on his knees, arms over his head, trying to block out the noise. Suddenly, there was a bright, blue-green flash—-and when the old-timer raised his head he saw the thing that was in his cabin!

"The old-timer's face twisted in fear when he gazed upon the unspeakably hideous apparition before him! Drum leaped to his feet, sprang toward the thing, barked once and fell dead—from sheer fright! The old-timer tore his eyes away from the awful specter and dashed to the cabin door. With trembling fingers he got the latch up, threw open the door and ran out into the storm.

He couldn't feel the cold rain or hear the crashing thunder as he ran through the woods; nor could he feel the wet tree branches that slapped across his face as he ran!"

My arm hairs were standing straight up as I stared at Tom, who was leaning forward in his chair, fingers gripping the leather arms. Then, he slumped against the back cushion and gazed intently at each of us before he spoke again. His voice was subdued and soft.

"They found the old-timer the next morning, walking along the dirt road that led to the highway. His clothes were shredded and his face was scratched and his eyes were wide and staring, staring at something too frightening to comprehend. They got him to the hospital in Harrison, and after they treated him for exposure, they had to put him in an old folks' home where people could care for him.

"He only spoke once after that night—and that was to tell me the true tale that I've just told you." Tom looked at us all for a moment before leaning forward to discard the butt of his cigar. And then, reaching into his vest pocket for a fresh one, he said, "Merry Christmas, all! Jud, let's go see if the ladies have any coffee left."

I'm still grateful to you, Jud, for having a friend like Tom.

Don

Dear Jud:

I need to replace the screen door on our back porch, which actually is a deck that I covered with corrugated roofing panels. On the west side, I had installed a screen door, thinking that I would screen in the rest of this porch. Well, Jud, 10 years have gone by and I haven't begun the screening-in project. Appropriately, I suppose, the screen door fell off its hinges not too long ago, apparently of its own accord. It had tumbled to the grass in a tangle of screen wire and rotted wood. I couldn't fault it for letting go after hanging there for years, exposed to the rain and hot Texas sun, feeling unneeded and neglected.

When I saw what had happened to my screen door, I stood for a moment staring at it, and I couldn't help comparing this poor example with Bernard Sutter's screen door, which not only banged against a real back porch, it picked up radio programs broadcast all the way from Springfield.

As you would recall, Bernard claimed that his screen door was a receiver for broadcasts transmitted by radio station KWTO. The door had no tuning apparatus, so Bernard wasn't able to listen to KGBX, the only other Springfield station in the early 1940s.

I don't know how many kilowatts KWTO beamed around our part of Missouri, but the station apparently had a powerful transmitter that blanketed many counties in southwest Missouri with big band music, country music, farm news, and war news. The station used their call letters as an acronym for their slogan: "Keep Watching The Ozarks." Obviously, Keep Watching The Ozarks would have made a better slogan for a television station than a radio station—but television hadn't come along yet.

The transmitter for Springfield's other radio station, KGBX, may have been too far from Republic, or too close, or there was something that had to do with the amplitude modulation. Whatever the reason, their signal wasn't detectable on Bernard's screen door. They suffered from another disadvantage, in my opinion. Their call letters made effective sloganeering virtually impossible. What do you do with "KGBX?" I don't believe I ever showed you my idea for a KGBX slogan: "<u>K</u>ing <u>G</u>eorge's <u>B</u>rother, <u>X</u>avier."

When you first told Bob and me about Bernard's famous door, we marveled at what magic it would be to listen to radio programs on our own back porch's screen door. I used to press my ear against the screen, hoping to hear an episode of *Jack Armstrong* or *Latitude Zero*. I'd have been glad to listen to news on the *National Farm and Home Hour*, or Ozarks hillbilly music played and sung by the Haden Family, or even the corny country humor of Goo Goo Rutledge. But all I ever heard was the sound of the wind passing through the tiny grid of the screen.

I did manage to hear a few minutes of H. V. Kaltenborn's news program crackling on the earphones of the crystal set you bought us. After I assembled the set, I took it down into the basement and attached the antenna to one of the water pipes. I moved the wire feeler over the crystal for hours, trying to pick up the sound of a broadcast. Finally, at noon one day, I heard Kaltenborn delivering war news in that funny clipped accent. Then, I clumsily jiggled the wire feeler and lost the station for good.

The most extraordinary thing to come through our back porch screen door was what I now believe must have been a ball of St. Elmo's Fire. I was sitting on the linoleum floor of the porch, near the door, watching an electrical storm outside. A bolt of lightning crashed, it seemed to me, right in our back yard. At the same time that the air around me crackled and the hair on my head and arms stood up, a bright, shimmering globe about the size of a softball passed through the screen wire and danced just above the floor for a few seconds. I could have reached out and touched the phenomenon if I hadn't been too terrified to move.

Isabel thought the stories about Bernard's screen-door radio were entertaining but she encouraged us not to repeat them. People already thought he was eccentric, she said. Some of the women at Hood Methodist Church told her that he sewed his own clothes, which was commendable but not usual for a farmer. She said that we should admire people like him "from afar."

Although I'd never been on Bernard's property, my mind could create a clear picture of him beside his screen door, listening. I could see him dragging a wooden kitchen chair onto the back porch at day's end, sitting next to the door, cocking his head toward the screen wire, and, with eyes closed, listening to news about the war, pork bellies, and commodity prices.

Bob and I weren't really that interested in technical explanations of the screen door phenomenon—how a wood frame with ordinary screen wire could function as a radio set, antenna and speaker all at once. That it happened was enough for us. At the barber shop, I asked Claude Bennett if he had ever listened to Bernard's screen door.

"I've never had the pleasure," said Claude. "He's never invited me out to his place." He said he wished he had a screen door like that for the barber shop. And then, nodding to the loafers sitting in a row of chairs against the wall, he said "If I did, and there was a way to turn up the dang volume on the thing, I wouldn't have to listen to these birds all day."

Claude swiveled the barber chair to turn his back on the grinning loafers, but I could still see them in the mirror. He went on to tell me what an amazing man Bernard was. He said that even in the winter, when it was too cold to sit out on an unheated back porch, Bernard didn't lack for entertainment.

Claude was using the hand clipper that pinched when he trimmed around my ears, and he said, "Why, when it gets too cold to use the screen door, old Bernard just sits by the wood stove in the kitchen and listens to music programs that come in on his gold tooth." He explained that the quality of radio broadcasts coming in on a tooth probably wouldn't be as good as what you'd hear on a screen door. In fact, he said, Bernard had mentioned that he couldn't make out words to the popular tunes he heard on his tooth, but he still enjoyed listening to the melody, tinny sounding as it was.

At one of my dentist appointments, I asked Doc Brim, who always reminded me of Raymond Massey, how Bernard could hear music coming from a gold tooth. Doc seemed to think about this for a moment, probably deciding how to explain such a phenomenon to a young boy, and then said that since the tooth was made of a rare metal, it somehow could pick up radio waves, and the programs were somehow sent through the jawbone to the ear drum. He said that if he ever got a chance, he would examine Bernard's tooth closely, and that perhaps he might even submit a paper about his findings to the *Dentist's Journal.* Then he unclipped the bib around my neck and said the words he always used when he had finished drilling and filling: "There y'go, Bub. Now don't eat nothin' for about an hour."

I've opened and closed many screen doors in the years since I left Republic. And I admit that I *have* actually tried listening to a few of them, so far without results. But it might happen someday. It might even happen on my new screen door, when I get it. A meteorite could land nearby, the impact having a cataclysmic effect on the atmosphere. A bizarre distortion of radio frequencies might result, and if the weave of my screen wire is just so, I could pick up the local public radio station. With luck, I might hear the music of Thomas L. Thomas, one of your favorites, or Yo Yo Ma, one of mine.

Yours for better listening,

Don

Life and Death Matters

> *A simple child*
> *That lightly draws its breath,*
> *And feels its life in every limb,*
> *What should it know of death?*

> —William Wordsworth

Dear Jud:

It took several seconds, as I lay in the dark in my bed, to recognize the sound that awakened me. Although I was snug and warm under my covers, all my hairs stood up when I heard it again: a man's voice, screaming. It came from far away, a long, hoarse, awful cry. Two more wild, terrible screams came through the darkness, and then it was still and quiet, as it always was at that time just before daybreak.

I turned so that I could face the haunted house across the field from our house. In the movie, *Third Dimension Murders*, a clawed, scabrous hand reaches toward the hero in one scene. After seeing that frightening movie, whenever Bob and I were alone at night on the enclosed back porch that served as our bedroom for a time, I was afraid that the hand, or one like it, would come from the haunted house and reach for me as I slept. So, after hearing the screams, I lay there, rigid, staring toward the window. But no fingernails tapped at the glass; there were no scrapes or rustles, and finally I slept.

In the morning, I mentioned the incident to you and Isabel, but neither of you had heard anything. At midmorning, though, you called Isabel to say that there had been a terrible accident during the night, and that was what I had heard.

A family lived in a small house on the street behind the Farmer's Exchange, near Dr. Mitchell's office. During the cold night, the father had gotten up to tend to the coal stove that heated their house. The embers had died down, so he added more coal, poured on some kerosene and tossed in a match to ignite it. The stove exploded and he was engulfed by the flaming fuel. He became a human torch, and in his panic, he ran from the house and down the street that paralleled the railroad tracks.

The man threw himself into a large mud puddle in a desperate attempt to douse the flames, but it was too late for him. When helpers came, they found him lying in the water. He died within a few minutes.

At the time I heard the poor man's agonized screams, I didn't realize I was hearing someone die. The end of life was a part of life I had not yet experienced, so death was still an abstraction to me. The only images of death I knew were the neat depictions of it I had seen in comic strips and books. When Dick Tracy plugged a gangster, his bullets left perfectly round, bloodless holes in the man's head. You could see daylight through the holes.

I had never seen a dead person, although I had seen a photo of a body. On my first visit to a classmate's house, I discovered a disturbing picture on the wall of the family's living room. It was a framed photo of my friend's grandfather lying in his casket. The open lid of the casket revealed the old man's gaunt profile, his eyes sunken and closed, and the beak of his nose sticking up prominently. I didn't know then that displaying photos of deceased family members was not uncommon at the turn of the century, and apparently it was a custom that a few people still observed in the 1940s.

The realization that death is inevitable—an inescapable fact of life—came slow to us, as it must among boys to whom life is essentially one diverting experience after another. And the way Doc Wiley died served as another lesson that life can end suddenly and unexpectedly.

We may have heard about the accident on the railroad tracks nearly as soon as you did, since it had occurred too far for you to see from your depot window and considering the speed at which bad news travels in small towns.

Doc Wiley was taking his usual shortcut to town across the tracks that summer morning. The old man was hard of hearing and never heard the warning blast of the speeding locomotive that hit him. The impact knocked him high into the air, a witness said, as high as the engine's smokestack. When he landed on the bed of the tracks, his body scooped out a longish crater that we rushed to look at as soon as we heard the news. As we inspected the oblong crater in the gravel of the railroad bed, the sight of it gave me an awful feeling. But that queasy moment passed, and for the remainder of the day we were self-important bearers of grim news, and capitalized on every opportunity to tell our friends about seeing "where Doc Wiley landed."

I felt important again when you took Bob and me to the scene of another fatal accident a year or so later. This one involved a Frisco passenger train derailment east of Republic near the area known as Little York. You felt obligated, as Republic's Frisco agent, to inspect the site and you allowed Bob and me to go with you—although you were at first reluctant, since you had heard that a passenger had been decapitated. When you used that word, it was the first time I had heard it, and you had to explain what it meant.

According to the reports you had received, when the coach car turned over on its side, a man occupying a window seat fell through the window and his head was sheared off. The coach car had been righted by the time we arrived, so there was not much for us to see. We walked along the roadbed beside the coach, and Bob and I studied the ground beneath the broken coach window to see if we could see the spot where the man's head would have rested. You said it wasn't proper to come looking for such a thing, and you led us away to view other scenes of the derailment.

It was several years after that before I actually gazed upon the face of a dead person. The shock of that moment was lessened by a circumstance that, to my relief, caused some giggling.

The deceased was Buddy Van Dusen. You knew his family. I knew him only well enough to speak when I met him on one of his strolls along Elm Street. Buddy had graduated from high school and was working somewhere out of town. He had been involved in an auto accident in which his car had traveled off the road and into a river. He was trapped inside and drowned, and many hours passed before the submerged car was spotted. When they pulled Buddy's car out of the water, they found his body in the back seat, arms extended toward the back window as if he had tried to break through it.

Buddy's body was taken to a funeral home, his arms still raised above his head. And the out-of-town mortician who prepared the body apparently was unable to bring the arms into the proper position of repose.

On the evening of the visitation, we joined the mourners and stood in line to see Buddy. He was dressed in a dark suit, with white shirt and tie, and didn't look that bad, considering what he had been through. But the way his arms were crossed over his chest was odd. His right arm lay against his suit, but the left arm, crossed over the right, was suspended an inch or so above his chest. Buddy appeared to be checking the time on his wristwatch. Amid snickering, I heard a voice whisper, "Wonder if Buddy's worried about bein' late in heaven?"

As observers of these small town tragedies, Bob and I remained, for the most part, safely distant and not personally affected by them. But that changed on a peaceful walk home from Sunday school during the summer of 1945. Bob and I were witnesses as death ceased to be an abstraction and became as real as the sidewalk under our feet.

You were still at church. Isabel was at home, cooking our big Sunday dinner. Bob and I had attended Sunday school at Hood Methodist Church and were walking past the lumberyard when the siren at the water tower started wailing. There was a fire somewhere. As we walked on, we smelled smoke and saw that it was coming from somewhere ahead of us on Elm Street.

We ran toward the smoke until we found the source: the rent house next to Tishy O'Dell's home. A man and woman were in the front yard, running in frantic patterns and looking toward the burning house. The woman clasped her hands together and shouted something. The man ran to the front door and disappeared in the thick smoke billowing from it. In a few moments, he staggered out, coughing, and fell to his knees on the grass. And as we watched this drama, I heard the screams of a child coming from inside the house.

I realized that the child had to be the sad-faced four- or five-year-old girl I had seen only the day before. She had stood in this same yard and watched me quietly as I walked by her house on my way to town. She and her parents had lived in the house for only a short time.

For several minutes, Bob and I were the only witnesses, but neighbors soon came running into the yard. Several women went to help the mother, and two men were struggling with the father, who had tried to run back into the inferno. And the little girl's screams were still coming from somewhere inside the house.

I heard the distinctive chugging made by Model T Ford engines and turned to see "Billy," Republic's ancient fire truck, pulling up with its crew of volunteer firemen. Billy had served as Republic's fire engine since 1922, and it was widely known that the old vehicle often had to be pushed or pulled to fire scenes. This day, the volunteers leaped from Billy and began to race about, tugging out a hose and hooking it to the hydrant on the corner. I remember this scene so well because it all seemed to take place in slow motion. The volunteer firemen were soon directing a stream of water onto the burning house, but by this time, the fire was out of control and flames were consuming the entire structure. And I no longer heard the little girl's cries.

Bill Hood's car rolled to a stop in the street, and you got out of the passenger side. When you reached Bob and me, your face was set in an expression I had never seen before. You looked both afraid and sad. As the heat from the fire became more intense, causing people to move further and further away, you said, "Come on, boys. Let's go home."

Isabel had fixed our favorite Sunday meal of fried chicken and mashed potatoes, but I couldn't eat a bite. I went into the backyard and climbed to my perch in the plum tree—a plank nailed to limbs high in the tree. This is where I came when I needed to contemplate a model ship–building project or a crush on a girl, or just to get away from Bob.

I gazed down at your neatly tended Victory Garden; the pasture beyond our property, where the Cantrell's cow was standing in a far corner; the Church of Christ beyond the pasture, from which came the voices of the congregation, still singing hymns a cappella.

Things appeared to be as they always were. Yet, I had the sensation of seeing things through an invisible shield of some sort and that I was separated from this familiar scene in a new way. The memory of that little girl's face kept returning to my mind.

I couldn't escape the thought that only the day before, I had walked right by her; and she had watched me with that sweet, sad look. She had stood there, absolutely unaware that in just a matter of hours she would be trapped inside her blazing home. Neither had I, when I had glanced at her, had any premonition that on the following morning I would be hearing her terrified cries as she died in that awful fire. I kept seeing the image of her sweet, small figure, standing by the sidewalk. I wished so that I had spoken to her, and I cried.

After the day's shocking events, I couldn't remember the lesson we had been given at Sunday school that morning. But that day provided another lesson, one that I kept not quite well enough in the years to come: when there is an opportunity to touch another person, if only with words, don't let it pass you by.

Don

Dear Jud:

As you walked home from work each evening, thinking, I imagine, about the good supper that awaited you and a quiet evening ahead with your pipe by the radio, you probably weren't aware of the four eyes directed toward you, tracking your approach.

From four blocks away, our figures might have been too small for you to see. But we could see you. More specifically, we could stand in front of our house and look down the sidewalk leading westward along Elm Street until we could see the figure of a walking man silhouetted by light from the setting sun.

We looked for a subtle but important sign: a signature walking style much like the loping gait that Leslie Howard exhibited as Ashley Wilkes in *Gone With the Wind*. That told us it was you. And if the shadow of your figure was uneven on one side, if it deformed into a lump at knee height, we knew you were carrying a burlap bag. If you were, a live chicken—perhaps two—would be inside the bag. And that was what all the surveillance was about. Chickens in the bag meant crispy, golden pan-fried chicken the next day.

I no longer could eat chicken after watching someone execute it. Fortunately, my mind protects me from the ghastly history of those ice-cold, plastic-wrapped packages of chicken parts at the supermarket. I don't think about that person far away, probably in Arkansas, who has taken care of the brutal, but necessary, first step. It also helps that the parts inside the package are so out-of-order it would be difficult to join them back together in the form of a chicken.

But when Isabel called you at the depot, you didn't go purchase a package at a supermarket. You would go to the back of the Farmer's Exchange, where it smelled of cattle feed and poultry feathers. And you would tell Bud Logan that you needed a chicken, or two chickens, depending on your orders. He'd then grab a chicken or two from the wire cages where they were kept and stuff them, flapping and squawking, into a burlap gunny sack. It wasn't fancy packaging, but it kept the birds from pecking your leg as you walked.

By the time you reached our house, we usually were circling you, begging you to let us look inside the bag. It was a morbid impulse. We knew what chickens looked like, but we wanted to stare at the doomed birds that jerked their heads and stared back at us one eye at a time.

The chickens usually spent the night in our cellar. I could stand in the kitchen, open the door to the cellar, and stare down into the darkness. The "fowl" odor would rise up the stairs and I'd hear the soft, questioning cluck of the chickens. Their "Cluck? Cluck?" must have meant, "Who's that? What's happening?"

Bob and I found your method of chicken-killing more riveting than Isabel's, since you were a neck-wringer and she favored the ax. To see you perform the act still wearing your necktie lent an incongruously formal aspect to the grisly scene.

Perhaps you never developed the knack for dressing casually because you spent so much of your day at work. You put on your shirt and tie in the morning, and that's what you wore for the rest of the day—even after work, pushing the plow in the Victory Garden. I'll bet you would remember, Jud, it was that sartorial habit that nearly claimed *your* neck the evening you tried to fix the washing machine wringer.

I was seated at the card table in the living room, struggling with those fiendish text-style math problems that I hated so, when I saw you walk into the kitchen and open the door to the cellar stairs. I thought no more about it until, sometime later, I heard Isabel say, "I wonder what's keeping Jud so long in the cellar?"

A few minutes later, I heard your footsteps as you climbed the stairs. You entered the kitchen, walked silently through the living room, and you might have reached your bedroom without

arousing any suspicions but for the odd, secret smile you wore—
and the jagged stub of the necktie that jutted from your collar.

After you reappeared, uncharacteristically dressed in a tie-less
shirt, open at the collar, you ruefully described how your tie got
caught in the washing machine wringer. You had replaced the
two cylindrical rubber rollers, and when you tried them out, they
grabbed your tie and pulled your chin down against the wringer
assembly. You said it was pulling pretty hard and things were
getting a little dim before you were able to pull your pocket knife
from your pocket, open it, and saw your tie off at the knot. It was
so like you to pretend that it wasn't really a close call.

When it was time for the chickens to meet their fate, you led
a small procession, with you and the chickens in the lead and
Bob and me following. When we reached the grassy area beside
the garden, the chickens, having sudden, dreadful premonitions,
began to squawk and flap their wings. Grasping one of the birds
by the neck, you planted your feet, legs bent slightly for balance in
the manner of a professional golfer about to putt, and you began
to crank your arms in a clockwise motion. Your arms whirled
strenuously, your necktie flapped wildly, and the bird became a
blur of white. When you released the chicken, it ran crazily for
a few seconds, its broken neck hanging down like a sock in a
puppy's mouth, not knowing yet it was dead.

Bob and I never wanted to try wringing a chicken's neck, but
we did try, unsuccessfully, to hang one. Filled with patriotic fervor
during those early WWII years, we, along with the Comisky
boys, pretended we were helping the FBI track down a brilliant
and dangerous German spy who could assume the appearance
of various animals. When our elite force caught him, he had
assumed the form of a chicken. On that same morning, we tried
the chicken, found it guilty of treason and sentenced it to death
by hanging.

We took the prisoner, as they say in English films, from
whence it was confined and from thence to the place of execution:
a long board between two stepladders. We solemnly placed the

chicken spy on the scaffold, put a hangman's noose around its neck, and pushed it off the plank. It fell a couple of feet before the rope jerked taut. When we inspected the bird, we found it to be unharmed but very angry. It pecked our hands when we removed the noose.

If you weren't available, Isabel handled the job of killing the chickens—which meant, of course, that there would be a minimum of ceremony and pageantry. She briskly marched the chickens out to the concrete slab where you burned our trash. There, she stretched a chicken on its side, held its legs with her left hand and brought an ax down on its neck with her right hand. Chunk! And that was it.

Murdering the chickens was only the first of a series of unsavory and messy steps that preceded a chicken dinner. After the killing, the birds were hung by their legs to be "bled" for a while. Then, the carcasses were plunged into a pot of hot water, which created a noxious odor but loosened the feathers so that they were easier to pluck. Once the skins were feather-free, Isabel removed the entrails, rinsed the nude chickens, and cut them into pieces. Only then were they ready for the frying pan. During this time, you had been in the garden digging the potatoes and picking the other vegetables that would accompany the entrée.

If we weren't too meddlesome, Isabel allowed us to stand close enough to the frying pan to breathe the aroma of those sizzling pieces. When, at last, the call to dinner came, we'd slam our bodies into our chairs, causing the old dining room table to pop and squeak—as did the weight of the steaming platters and bowls it supported. The centerpiece, of course, was the fried chicken, golden and crispy and fragrant. We noisily claimed our favorite pieces and took servings from the other dishes that were circulating: mashed potatoes, brown gravy, peas, corn on the cob, slices of beefsteak tomatoes—all fresh from your garden.

The chicken pieces were quickly reduced to a pile of bones. And then our unsightly plates were taken away and replaced by smaller plates holding pieces of warm apple or raisin pie. Isabel allowed us to have a third of a cup of coffee, creamed and sugared, with our pie.

At the end of the meal, you went to your green chair and the rest of us cleared the table. Bob and I usually milled around and bumped into things until we were ordered to stand aside by our sisters. When that activity subsided, we took towels and helped dry the plates and glasses and silverware.

After one of those meals, Bob and Patty and I were left at the sink, finishing the dishes. Patty saw me staring out the kitchen window toward the area where the chickens had met their fate. She said, "One of these days, you'll be old enough to help kill the chickens. Think you'll want to do that?"

As children do, I said, "I don't know." But I did know then, and still know now. I wouldn't.

Don

The Weezer Bug

Dear Jud:

The cicadas in the elm, ash, and maple trees on our Missouri street played a song different from the sound I hear from cicadas now. Can it really be that there are regional differences in the love songs these creatures perform for each other? It must be so.

The cicadas in Houston's trees produce a monotonous buzzing compared to the mesmerizing, two-note tune we listened to every summer evening. Anyone who heard this tune would understand why we called these insects "weezer bugs." I liked to lie alone on a blanket in our front yard and listen to them. I'd let my ears single out one bug from the hundreds I could hear, and listen as it began its call, which rose in volume and then plaintively faded away: *weezer, weezer, weezer, weezer, weeeeezzzerrrrr.*

This odd little song was repeated in intervals of their own choosing by all the other weezer bugs. It was a wonderful racket and perfect accompaniment for viewing the spectacular show of stars in the clear night sky. Lying there, smelling your pipe smoke drifting down from the porch and the warm, grassy odor of the blanket, I'd watch for shooting stars and wonder what they were. Then I'd fix my gaze on one of the millions of stars in the black dome above me, and if I stared at it long enough, it would appear to be suspended in a dark pool of endless depth.

During that moment of special awareness, I could almost feel the movement of the earth as it turned and turned through the same night sky that held the stars. I would feel as though I might soar right off our lawn and into the sky. Then I'd wrap myself in a blanket cocoon and breathe its earthy fragrance and listen to the reassuring sound of the weezer bugs.

I had seen many of the empty, amber-hued shells clinging to the bark of trees, and I knew that weezer bugs came from these husks. But I was somewhat disappointed when I saw my first genuine, living weezer bug. I was high in my favorite of the three ash trees that grew in front of our house. A short raspy noise sounded near me and on a limb nearby I saw the insect. I had expected to see something that looked more like a katydid. But this bug was bigger than my thumb. The creature's blunt head had wide-set, bulging eyes.

Its body was thick and greenish-black in color, and the folded, transparent wings extended past its tail. I knew this was a weezer bug because I had seen something like it emerging, not-quite formed yet, from an amber husk. I reached toward the weezer bug, and when my finger touched it, it buzzed loudly and launched itself explosively from the tree limb.

Later in the summer, we began to find weezer bugs lying dead under the trees. We held the dead bugs between our fingers and sailed them through the air, shouting "weezer, weezer!" And it was during one of these games that one of the boys observed that a weezer bug's head reminded him of Kenneth Halpern.

I was afraid of Kenneth. We all were. It was the way he looked, with his flat nose and wide-set eyes and misshapen mouth; and the way he staggered down the street, hunched over, arms jerking and fingers curling and uncurling. People called him a "spastic." I didn't know what that meant, and I didn't know why he was the way he was. I had never heard of diseases that can do what had been done to Kenneth. I just knew that the sight of him filled me with dread. And I suppose it was bravado that made us all believe it was funny to call him the "Weezer Bug."

I had heard his wild cry coming from the Halperns' house and had shuddered at the gurgling sound he made the first time I had come face-to-face with him downtown. On another occasion, I was riding my bicycle illegally on the sidewalk in front of LaVerne Claiborn's drug store. Just as I coasted near the door, it burst open and the Weezer Bug lurched onto the sidewalk in front of me. He whirled toward me and a loud "Glaaaa!" came from his rubbery mouth. It frightened me so, I jerked my handlebars to the right and my bike crashed over the curb, spilling me onto the street. I didn't even feel the abrasions when my knees and arms scraped against the pavement. I was so terrified, I jumped to my feet, snatched my bike, and pushed it as fast as I could away from Claiborn's. When I reached the railroad tracks, I turned to see if the Weezer Bug was chasing me. But I saw him far in the distance, moving unsteadily beyond the drug store, heading, like me, for home.

My feelings about the Weezer Bug began to change one afternoon while I was at home with a bad cold. Bob was at school, Isabel had gone to town on a shopping expedition, and I was alone in the house.

I was tired of lying in bed, so I got up, wandered into the living room, and looked out one of the small windows beside the fireplace. The hairs on my arms stood up when I saw a figure I recognized. It was the Weezer Bug, lurching along the sidewalk in the next block, on our side of Elm Street, moving toward our house. For a moment, I was so frightened I felt sick to my stomach, thinking he had learned that I was home alone and was coming to get me.

The Weezer Bug was in front of Ab Norman's house, at the corner of Elm and Hampton. He stopped and gazed about, seeming unsure of where to go next. I held my breath, waiting to see what he would do. To my immense relief, he turned and began to make his way back toward town.

At that point, Lynn Martin's green DeSoto pulled to a stop on Hampton and turned right on Elm Street. Lynn must have spotted the Weezer Bug on the sidewalk in front of Ab's house; he stopped the car and I could see him leaning over to push the passenger side door open. Lynn was offering a ride to the Weezer Bug, who stopped and turned toward the DeSoto. I saw that he understood Lynn's offer, because he stepped off the sidewalk and moved erratically toward the two-by-twelve-inch plank that Ab had placed across the deep ditch that paralleled Elm Street.

Lynn sat motionless in his car, watching as the Weezer Bug stepped onto the plank. He probably was anticipating what was about to happen, just as I was. The Weezer Bug somehow reached the mid-point of the plank, then his unreliable legs staggered over the edge and he fell into the ditch. He scrambled to his feet and attempted to crawl up the side of the ditch nearest Lynn's DeSoto, but his feet couldn't gain purchase and he tumbled to the bottom of the ditch again.

I giggled at the spectacle, but then, as the poor figure struggled in the ditch, I began to see it not as the fearsome Weezer Bug, but as Kenneth Halpern, a terribly afflicted boy trying and failing to perform what would have been an easy feat for me. I found myself rooting for him to conquer the ditch. Again, he tried; again, he rolled back into the ditch. Lynn, seeing that Kenneth couldn't climb out alone, jumped into the ditch to help. He grasped Kenneth under one arm and used the other hand to push the seat of the boy's pants until he reached the street level. Then, Lynn climbed the side of the ditch, helped Kenneth into the car and the two drove away toward town.

I watched until I couldn't see the DeSoto anymore, and I realized that my dread and fear were gone. What I felt instead was a mixture of sadness and guilt. I don't say that Kenneth and I became friends from that moment on. We didn't. I still found him hard to look at, and I tried to stay away from him. But I did quit calling him "the Weezer Bug."

Don

Dear Jud:

You didn't know about Eddie Byers until our seventh-grade teacher discovered his secret. Before that momentous event, if you'd noticed him at all, his was one of those faces that would have been at the fringe of the group of boys that often gathered in front of our house. You'd have seen a pleasant-looking boy, thin like me, standing quietly, watching more than participating.

That was the thing about Eddie. I never really got to know him well, but he seemed different to me from the first. There was something about him that I first mistook as sadness. As we became better acquainted, I understood that what set Eddie apart from the rest of our friends was more an air of distraction and that was the reason for the customary dreamy look on his face. He seemed always to be thinking about something else. (And after his secret was revealed, we understood what it was that Eddie was always thinking about.)

I don't believe you ever met Eddie's father. The Byers family—actually, it was just the father, Eddie, and his sister; Eddie never mentioned his mother—moved to the Republic area in 1946, just in time for Eddie to enroll in the seventh grade.

Eddie's sister was fifteen years old and entered the freshman class at Republic High School. The Byers rented a house in Little Italy, which, as you often pointed out, was the north side neighborhood distinguished primarily by the absence of Italians in residence. Before the Byers moved to town, I only knew one person who lived in Little Italy. That was Mr. Fischer, and he probably hated Italians. He was that cranky old Spanish–American War veteran we used to torment because we knew that it infuriated him if we touched his front fence. It was always entertaining to ride our bikes to Little Italy to see if Mr. Fischer was on his front porch. If he was, we gathered on the sidewalk in front of his house as if to hold a powwow. We let our bicycles bang against his wrought-iron fence, and we slouched against the fence, letting our arms dangle carelessly over it. This caused him to haul himself stiffly from the porch swing and dodder down the steps toward us, shouting, "You boys go away! You're touching my fence! You have no right to touch my fence!"

I feel certain you'd have heard from Mr. Fischer if he could have seen well enough to identify us.

But, back to Eddie. He seemed to enjoy being part of our group although he was never really an active participant in our boy doings. When we played softball, he sat in the grass and watched. He'd look on as we drew a circle in the dirt for a game of marbles, but he didn't join in. He preferred to doodle in the black notebook he always carried.

I began to notice two things about Eddie. When he sat near us as a spectator, he conveyed mild interest in what we were doing. But if girls were nearby, he quit watching us and stared at them. The other habit was even more intriguing. When he was working in his notebook, he closed it quickly when someone approached. I wondered what he was writing or drawing that he didn't want anyone to see.

We learned the secret of that notebook not too many weeks into the school year. And the way the secret was discovered was quite sensational.

It happened during seventh-grade history. I, myself, was day-dreaming and sketching one of the square-rigged sailing ships that I loved so. Eddie was sketching, too, and didn't hear the sound of Mrs. Spiller's feet on the hardwood floor behind him. I had just looked in Eddie's direction, and saw her bend forward, clutching at Eddie's shoulder. I heard her gasp and say, "Eddie! My God! What are you doing?"

He slammed the notebook closed and tried to slide it out of sight. But Mrs. Spiller grabbed it and pulled him to his feet. She hustled him down the aisle, scolding and threatening, and they clamored out of the classroom. We all sat there for a few minutes, too surprised even to laugh.

During recess, we heard rumors that Eddie Byers had been caught with a notebook full of drawings of naked women. By lunch, we were hearing an even better rumor: the pictures of the naked ladies had been drawn by Eddie.

He wasn't at school for the rest of the week, and some of the girls said that he had been expelled. But our teachers provided the official explanation: he had been reprimanded by the principal and sent home for the remainder of the week, but he would be back in class on Monday.

I saw Eddie again on Monday morning. He was standing alone on the grounds behind the grade school building. Several girls stood together a distance away, pretending not to look at him but furtively glancing at him, whispering, and giggling.

One by one, boys walked up to stand with him, and I joined them. We asked Eddie if we could look at his notebook. But he told us that he had been made to give it to his father, and that his father really wasn't all that angry about the incident. "He doesn't care what I do," Eddie said.

Could he get the notebook back? Sure, he said. So we made arrangements to meet him the next afternoon in the abandoned garage on Bill McClure's property. This was convenient for Bob and me, since our house was just across the field from there.

When school let out the next day, we crossed the tracks near the depot. I looked toward your office windows facing the tracks, but couldn't see you. I wondered what you would think if you knew that we were on our way to look at pictures of women without any clothes on. But I didn't let that thought deter me as we made our way to the old garage. It was a while before Eddie arrived because he had to walk all the way to Little Italy, retrieve the notebook from his house, and walk back to our street.

Before long, we heard footsteps, and there was Eddie, standing at the door of the garage. He came inside and we eagerly gathered around him as he opened his secret book. It became very quiet in the garage, and the reverent silence was broken only by the rhythmic rustle of turning pages and Gerald Whittington's noisy breathing. Gerald's habit of breathing through his mouth annoyed me even more than usual.

Eddie's book was a revelation. On each page was a full-length drawing of a youngish woman wearing not a stitch. I had seen cartoon drawings of a naked female only once before. In this very garage, Dizzy Watts had shown several of us his Big Little book, which contained a bootleg and pornographic version of a comic strip featuring Popeye, Olive Oyl, and Wimpy.

As we stared at the drawings, I thought about my own secret: in the presence of a clergyman, I had once stolen a look at Lorraine Cowan's almost-bare chest—or at least a side view of it. During the previous summer, the Baptists had extended an invitation to Bob and me and several others to spend a week at a church camp in Arkansas, and you and Isabel had granted us permission to go. The Baptist preacher and his wife drove us to the camp, and Lorraine sat between Bob and me in the backseat.

She was two grades ahead of us in school, and we didn't know her well. She seemed to find Bob entertaining, however, which was a relief. If he hadn't been in the car I wouldn't have known what to say to her. At one point, Lorraine leaned forward to rest her arms on the back of the front seat. It was summer, and she was wearing a loose-fitting cotton top with large armholes. I happened to glance to my left and found myself staring at her right breast. Most of it was concealed by the bra she was wearing, but still, this was my first look at a live girl in lingerie. My eyes riveted on her.

She had no idea she was being so accommodating, which made me feel guilty about what I was doing. Staring at her with my head facing toward the front and my eyes swiveled hard to the left, I began to worry that my eyes might lock into that position and I'd have to go through life cockeyed. But I couldn't stop staring. And over the next several days at the church camp, the image of Lorraine kept popping into my mind, particularly during the Bible study class on the subject of begetting, during which the instructor, in his nasal, whiny voice, droned endlessly about how Azariah begot Amariah, and Amariah begot Ahitub, and Abitub begot Zadok, and so on, and so on. At night, I prayed to God to forgive me for thinking about Lorraine's chest so much.

As we bounced along in the car, my eyes still fixed on Lorraine, I was jarred by the sound of the preacher's voice: "*That's* what I've been wanting you to see!" I jumped and sheepishly tore my eyes away to glance at the preacher. I was surprised and relieved to see that he was looking at neither Lorraine nor me but was nodding out his window toward a barnyard we were passing. Through our side window, I could see a man trotting on a path that circled the entire barnyard.

"I've heard about that fellow," said the preacher. "He's not quite right in the head. Thinks he's a racehorse." As the farm passed from our view, the preacher explained that the trotting man was mentally disturbed and actually believed he was a racehorse: not a jockey but a thoroughbred race horse. According to reports the preacher had heard, the man trotted around and around on that circular path every day, rain or shine.

During our week at the church camp, I forgot about the trotting man. But we traveled the same highway on our return to Republic. It was raining when we passed that barnyard again. And, as if God were proving that preachers don't lie, there was the man, dressed in a yellow slicker, trotting in a circle in the rain.

But back to the garage, where we were assessing Eddie's skill as an artist. His sketches were far superior to the crude representations that had been scraped into the walls of the boys' restroom at school. The female figures he had drawn were not just buxom and shapely, but graceful, too. The arms and legs were slender, and the waists and hips were pleasantly proportioned. What impressed me most, however, was Eddie's obvious knowledge of the female anatomy.

I wondered how he had obtained that knowledge, because my own information was scanty. It wasn't like you to sit Bob and me down to have "the talk." You may have intended to, but I suspect that your upbringing made this sort of thing difficult. The truth is, Jud, listening to you explain the facts of life would have embarrassed me more than you. In any case, Bob and I eventually managed to learn what we needed to know from both suspect and reliable sources.

Eddie was far ahead of his peers in that respect. When he turned the last page of drawings that afternoon and closed his notebook, someone asked Eddie how he knew so much about girls. And someone else said, "Yeah, how do you know they really look like that?" That produced some elbowing and chuckling.

Eddie said, "Because I've seen them." He explained that his father kept a folder full of pictures of naked ladies in a dresser drawer. After Eddie discovered them, he began to take them out while his father was at work, and he practiced drawing from them. We asked him if he had ever seen a real girl that way. He said he had and that one girl had allowed him to draw a picture of her. This had happened before the Byers moved to Republic.

Well, Jud, at that point Eddie had to leave so that he could get home to do chores his father had instructed him to do. I watched him stroll away from the garage, and I wondered how he could be so untroubled by trouble that would have devastated me.

For a week or so, Eddie was a celebrity, or at least a curiosity, at school. Among the boys, he was venerated for his forbidden knowledge of girls. But there was something unsettling about Eddie's familiarity with female topography. I never would have admitted it, but I think I just didn't want that mystery to be solved yet.

Eddie moved away from Republic in 1948. I saw him at school a day or so before the Byers left town, but he didn't say goodbye or even mention that they were moving.

I haven't thought about Eddie for years, but it would be interesting to know what happened to him. Did he graduate from high school? Did he convert his artistic ability into a rewarding career? Perhaps he became a producer of adult films somewhere. Or an art director at an advertising agency.

In the days after Eddie's secret was revealed, some of Bob's cronies reported that there was much speculation among the brain trust at Juggy's Place on what would become of Eddie. I liked your idea best, Jud. Even Isabel laughed when you predicted that Eddie would become a bookkeeper, since he was so good at figures.

Don

Dear Jud:

If I had known what a terrifying experience it would prove to be, I'd have had no part in the plan to frighten Ida Wiley out of her wits.

That event, which is still troubling to recall, took place on Halloween night during the year Bob and I turned sixteen. We and several friends were roaming the streets of Republic, searching for bird baths, lawn chairs, and other movable objects that could be taken from yards and porches and relocated elsewhere in town. We had broken out several street lights on Elm Street and were walking toward our house when we saw Ida's small house next to the funeral home. That's when the scheme was hatched.

When Ida's husband died, she sold their home and had a small cottage built on the lot adjacent to the funeral home. Her late husband, a retired large-animal veterinarian, was one of many men known in Republic as "Doc." You once commented that in our town, use of that title didn't necessarily require a medical degree. There was the late Doc Wiley, the vet; Doc Leidinger, the MD; Doc Mitchell, the osteopath; the late Doc Beal, the MD who set my broken arm; Doc Brim, the dentist; Doc O'Dell, the druggist; and Doc French, the Chevrolet dealer.

I had always been fond of Ida, whose bearing reminded me of those patrician society ladies in the Abbott and Costello movies, but who also became gushy in the manner of Billie Burke when she spoke to Bob and me. She had professed to adore Bob and me from the time we were twin babies. When we pressed her, Isabel would retell the story of Ida's reaction when she first saw us as infants, lying side-by-side in our king-size baby buggy. She clasped her hands to her breast, Isabel said, and cried, "Oh! Precious lumps of gold!"

On that Halloween night, the light in one window told the lumps of gold and their friends that Ida was still awake. We agreed that we should hide in the darkness and make horrifying ghoulish sounds that would convince an elderly woman, all alone, that hideous fiends were outside her house and were about to come in.

We ran through the night and flattened ourselves in the grass at the edge of her property, our backs toward the funeral home. I glanced over my shoulder at the dark windows of the building behind us, which seemed somewhat more ominous than usual. I had never liked being this close to the funeral home. It was a place we had always feared passing by at night—a dread owing to the fact that this was a place to which the dead were brought. None of us would admit to believing in ghosts. But at the same time, when walking by late on a windy night, it was hard to doubt that this was the place where dwelled the spirits of those who had been brought up the long ramp that led to the back entrance.

As I lay on my stomach, facing Ida's house, I remembered stories I had heard about the house behind me. One story told how, years before the house had been converted into a mortuary, a despondent woman living there had killed herself—possibly in the very room that overlooked us now. According to the story, the woman had sat in a chair, barefoot; placed the muzzle of a shotgun in her mouth; and pulled the trigger with one of her toes.

The wind had picked up, and over the sighing in the branches overhead, I heard feet running. I looked up to see one of our party dashing toward Ida's lighted window. He crouched low, dragged his fingernails across the window screen and uttered a low moan that broke and became an awful, ululating wail. We joined in with a chorus of gibbering shrieks and hoarse grunts. I envisioned poor Ida inside, clasping her hands to her breast in terror. But instead, I was surprised to see the porch light come on, illuminating Ida's frail figure in the doorway. She hesitantly opened the screen door a few inches and in her Billie Burke voice, spoke into the night, "Hello? Who's there? Is someone there?"

Ida was spunkier than I had expected. She continued to stand in the doorway as we unleashed another series of hellish screams to frighten her back inside. It seemed that we succeeded, because she stepped back inside and a light went on in another window.

The wind seemed cooler, and I turned to glance again at the funeral home. It seemed closer to us than it had a moment ago.

I heard a clumping noise. Someone had found some walnuts and was bouncing them on Ida's roof. This brought her to the doorway again, and this time she ventured out onto her small porch. "Who is it?" she asked of the night. "Who's there?"

I heard some conspiratorial snickers, and then I felt a tingling on my back. I looked behind me again—and I swear that the funeral home appeared to be nearer than it had been even a moment earlier. It must have been my overheated imagination, but the side of the building seemed to loom over me. And what was that pale shape in one of the dark windows? Was it a reflection from Ida's porch light? Or was it a woman's face? Every hair on my body sprang up as if I had walked into a magnetic field; the air around me seemed taut, the way it might feel to be surrounded by static electricity.

Our moaning and wailing had stopped. The others seemed to sense something, too. I saw the shadowy figure of someone in our group turn and look behind us. I turned to look, too, and in my state of mind it seemed that the side of the funeral home was closer yet—almost as if it were advancing upon us. And the pale, oval shape was still in the dark window. I heard someone whisper, "Hey, guys! I think we'd better go!" And another voice whispered, "Yeah, let's get the hell out of here!"

Ida stepped back inside and closed her door just as we scrambled to our feet and ran. As I began to run, I glanced toward the funeral home. The building now appeared be in its proper location, and I no longer could see the pale, oval shape in the window. Even so, I don't believe I have ever been more terrified than I was at that moment. My skin was crawling and my back was tingling as I ran as fast as I could out into the street and on toward town. Our group ran together, without uttering a sound until we reached Main Street. We stopped near the library to catch our breath, and only then did we begin to laugh sheepishly and make feeble jokes about how frightened Ida must have been.

When our group broke up, Bob and I decided to take the long way home on streets that wouldn't take us past Ida's house or the funeral home. We walked all the way to the high school, down the road past Lynn Martin's house, and across the field into our backyard. The moon came out from behind the clouds as we climbed the back steps to the porch, and I glanced down Elm Street toward town. Two blocks away, in the moonlight, I could see the funeral home; at that moment our familiar back porch had never looked so good to me. Just as I was about to open the screen door to step inside, a sudden chill rose in the dark and brushed against me.

I know that it must have been just a cool nocturnal breeze. But on that night, who would have blamed me for wondering if it was something else?

Don

Dear Jud:

I never told you about shooting that spider with my new .22-caliber rifle. Bob and I had had enough trouble assuring you and Isabel that if you allowed us to have rifles, there'd be nothing to worry about. We gave you names of other gun-owning boys in town who were far less responsible than we. And we promised earnestly that we wouldn't try to puncture the water tower with our bullets, as Harold Gene Boggs had done; or fire even a single shot within the city limits of Republic.

The credentials we provided didn't mention the BB gun battle in the Hideout, that brushy hill on the east side of town, during which Bob barely missed being blinded in one eye or the other. Our gang was pursuing another similarly armed gang when one of them got off a shot that left a neat BB-sized depression just above the bridge of Bob's nose. If the BB had struck half an inch to the right or left, it would have found an eyeball. It was lucky for both of us that the small dent had pretty much disappeared by the time you got home from work so we didn't have to tell you he'd been poked with a stick.

Nor did we ever tell you and Isabel that Bob had used his BB gun to shoot Ab Norman in the buttocks. Bob was walking past Ab's house one morning when he spotted Ab, who was loading empty twenty-gallon milk cans into his Missouri Farmer's Association dairy truck. When Ab bent over, his blue overalls stretched tightly across the cheeks of his rear, presenting a target that Bob was unable to resist. Ab said he thought a hornet had stung him until he turned and saw Bob holding the BB gun. He never reported Bob's sneak attack to you, nor, I'm sure, did he tell you about his revenge. Some days later, he enticed Bob into helping him load some of those heavy milk cans, and, once Bob had climbed inside the refrigerated compartment of the truck, Ab slammed the door shut and left Bob inside, in the dark, just long enough to make an impression.

Without the above information, you and Isabel eventually relented and said we could have the rifles if we were careful and used good sense. That's why I wasn't eager for you to know about the spider. I feared that my using a rifle to hunt spiders might not, in your view, represent good sense.

After we had taken possession of our new rifles, Bob and I thought you probably would take us out in the country and teach us what you knew about firearms. You made sure we understood the basic firearm safety procedures that came with our rifles, but beyond that, you said, you had no experience with rifles and hunting. We had seen the little snub-nose .22-caliber pistol that you kept in the top drawer of the bureau in your bedroom. Once, when you and Isabel weren't around, we had opened the drawer and unfolded the purple, velvety fabric you'd wrapped around the pistol, and we stared at it with awe. When we asked Isabel why you kept the little pistol, she said she wasn't sure and that you had never fired it and really had no use for it, but just hated to throw it away.

So, we were disappointed when you said you'd allow us to have the rifles, but that you didn't think that sneaking up on animals and killing them was much of a sport. I didn't want to hear that then, but it's a sentiment I share with you today.

If you had misgivings about my skill as a marksman, your instincts were true. Although I did manage to shoot that spider and some years later bag a duck with a .30-06 deer rifle, I was never a good shot. I have unpleasant memories of my time on the firing range during Naval Reserve boot camp. A gunner's mate watched me fire several rounds toward the target and announced—too loudly, I thought—that I was the worst shot he'd ever seen. And on a Naval Reserve training cruise on Lake Superior, when it was my turn to fire a 20 mm cannon at a target being towed by a destroyer escort, the first round I fired splashed only yards away from our own ship. The next two rounds missed the target by at least a quarter of a mile. If I had been one of those sailors standing by the rail on the destroyer escort, I'd have been more than a little uneasy.

Hitting that spider was a different matter, although I didn't start the day intending to shoot one. It just became a target of opportunity, only the second opportunity of the day as it turned out. After you had gone to the depot one cool, fall morning, I decided to take my new .22 rifle and go rabbit hunting. I rushed through breakfast so that I could have plenty of time to bag my limit. My plan was to hike the fields south of Republic and bring home a rabbit—maybe several—to show you. I was such a novice that I didn't know I stood practically no chance of hitting a darting rabbit with a bolt-action, single-shot .22. Unencumbered by this knowledge, I proceeded happily with my plans. I wrapped a sandwich in wax paper, put on my wool mackinaw, and went hunting.

I'd chosen a beautiful fall day for my hike across the fields. I kept the rifle unloaded and the barrel pointed downward while walking, as I'd promised. And when I came to a fence row, I put my rifle on the other side of the fence before climbing over. I walked for a while before I sighted a clump of golden weeds which I had heard other boys call "rabbit weed." I had never actually seen a rabbit residing in this kind of weed before, but I assumed that it must be called by this name for good reason. So, I knelt down, slipped a .22 bullet in the chamber and waited for my first rabbit to emerge. Nothing happened. I began to hike again, rifle at the ready, all of my senses in a heightened state. But after scouring the fields for several hours, not one rabbit did I see.

By noon, I was getting tired, hungry, and discouraged. I had reached a wooded area not far from Otho Bridge's farm, and when I saw a crow on a bare branch of one of the trees, I sighted on him, fired, and missed. This nevertheless disturbed him, and he cawed irritably to warn other crows—several of which cawed back in what I took to be jeering tones.

I found a comfortable-looking spot under a walnut tree and sat down. When I took the wax paper wrapping from my sandwich, the bread was mashed flat and limber, and I found that sandwiches in this condition lose a good deal of their flavor. I ate it anyway, which made me thirsty. But I'd brought nothing to drink. I leaned back to stare at the sky, and noticed that clouds were moving in. I wondered if I might get rained on during my hike back to town and thought about heading back. Instead, I surrendered to a pleasantly dozy feeling and closed my eyes.

I suppose that the possibility of rain was on my mind, because in that drowsy, slightly giddy state I remembered a very satisfying bike ride through heavy rain a few years earlier. I had ridden to the depot to visit you on a gray spring day. On my ride home, it had begun to sprinkle; by the time I was halfway home, I was in a downpour. I was wearing a leather aviator helmet equipped with goggles—the style of helmet worn by our fighter pilots—so I flipped down the goggles to shield my eyes from the rain. As I leaned far over the handlebars, pumping my legs rhythmically, I thought how heroic I must look to anyone watching from an Elm Street window. I squinted my eyes and set my mouth in a grim line as I pushed heedlessly through the punishing rain.

Lying under the walnut tree, my mind flowed from that memory to another fantasy in which I was rescuing Veronica Lake, my favorite hapless beauty. In this adventure, I was a restless yet likable wanderer wearing the same helmet and goggles and riding my bicycle across the Golden Gate Bridge. Ahead, on the bridge's roadway, I saw a commotion, and my acute vision revealed that a brutish Nazi Gestapo thug was attempting to throw Miss Lake from the bridge. I poured on the speed, and before the Nazi Gestapo thug was aware of me, I slammed my bicycle into him, sending him staggering. I leaped from my steed and caught Miss Lake in my left arm while, with my right, I delivered a tremendous uppercut that sent the Nazi over the rail and into the shark-infested waters far below. And as I gently set the beautiful actress on her feet, she looked into my eyes and said, "Ohhh, you're so wonderful!"

Fortunately, a fly walking on my nose awakened me, forestalling what was always the awkward part of this recurring daydream: not knowing what to say to a girl, even the woman I loved.

I opened my eyes and stared upward. High above, suspended among bare tree branches, a fairly large spider was silhouetted against the now gray sky. Somehow, the spider had managed to string a web between the branches of my tree and the tree adjacent. The circular loops of the web formed a target and the spider, at the center, was the bull's-eye.

There had been only one opportunity to shoot my new .22 rifle that day, and spiders had always frightened me, so I decided to test my aim on this one. I sighted on the spider and fired. I missed. I tried again and missed again. But on the third shot, the spider disappeared. I had expected the impact of the .22 projectile to cause a splattering of some sort, but my target literally just vanished in the fall air. I thought about my kill and felt good at first. I hated spiders.

The wind was picking up, and I decided to start back, not wanting to slog home through a rainstorm. I picked up my rifle and retraced the route that had brought me to this spot in the woods. As I walked, the image of the spider on its web again came to mind. I began to feel a little sorry for what I had done to the poor, unsuspecting creature that had worked so hard to build a safe home high in the trees.

I decided not to say anything about shooting the spider, especially to you. Trudging along, I thought about how an interrogation might go—the pointed, probing questions that could lead me to blurt out what I had done. So, I tried to prepare myself for your questioning.

"Get anything, Don?" you might ask, requiring me to say yes, or lie and say no. And if I did lie and say no, you would eye me questioningly and ask, "Not *any*thing?" And I would have to look away and say, "No, not a single thing."

My face must have shown how relieved I was when, at supper that evening, you simply asked me if I'd had a good time on my outing. I was able to say I had. And when you asked if I'd bagged any rabbits, I was able to answer, "Nope."

By the time supper ended, I was feeling pretty good about my day. My responses to your questions had been accurate, if not rich with details, and I hadn't shot any farm animals or water towers. Only a spider. And no one likes spiders.

Don

Dear Jud:

I still don't like to think about the way it felt the night I stepped on Howard Toth's stomach. It was yielding and spongy, and it moved beneath my foot. When I jerked my foot away, a voice from the darkness below, coming from somewhere near the stomach, said, almost casually, "Better go in there, boy, and get the glory of the Lord in your soul."

We were both beneath one of the windows of the Assembly of God church. I gathered that whoever it was down there by my feet—it sounded like Howard—had been taking part in the worship service inside and, overcome by the Spirit, had come outside to lie down until he was steady enough to go back inside.

I squinted down into the darkness and saw a shadowy figure preparing to stand upright. Then it moved into a beam of light from the church window, and I saw that it was, in fact, Howard. He glanced at me as if nothing had happened, and walked briskly away into the night.

Howard apparently never said anything to you, because you never mentioned that incident. Perhaps he would have been embarrassed for you to know what had happened to the man who hung the canvas bags of mail from the mast beside the main line tracks. If Bob and I happened to be at the depot at the right time, we could watch as the big hook on the baggage car of the Springfield-bound passenger train plucked the mailbag from the mast.

We sometimes followed behind Howard as he used a pushcart to transport the big canvas mailbag from the post office to the tracks. He was a small, slightly built man, but he seemed to handle the heavy mailbag with ease. When we reached the mast, he would unfold its metal arms and extend them toward the tracks. Then he'd grab the top of the mailbag, climb several steps on the mast's built-in ladder, and snap the bag to the end of the top arm. Jumping down, he'd secure the other end of the bag to the bottom arm. Then we would wait for the train to come.

It was always thrilling to watch the train round the curve west of the depot, blowing its whistle alarmingly as it approached the Main Street intersection. The locomotive and coal tender would hurtle past, then the baggage car with the large hook-like device extending from the door. As soon as the hook snagged the mailbag a man inside the baggage car pulled a lever to quickly draw the speeding hook and its burden into the car.

What would you have thought if I had told you about stepping on Howard outside the Assembly of God church? You'd have wondered what I was doing, creeping around the churchyard in the dark.

One of the older boys had told Bob that listening to the "holy rollers" was worthwhile. So, one night, we and several friends crept through the darkness toward the Assembly of God church, hoping to see and hear the multitude inside speak in tongues. As I neared the window, I could hear them shouting "Yalla balla voballa alla katalla!" or words to that effect.

While we were listening to the alien syllables of the unknown tongue, you and Isabel probably were sitting on the front porch, talking softly and listening to other music—the songs of the insects at night. People who haven't lived in a small town in a time before television may not have experienced the calming effect of an insect chorus. And they would no doubt be surprised to know what boys of that time would do for diversion—even go to church. You, on the other hand, recognized that in Republic, the alternatives to churchgoing were few, and you probably hoped fervently that something good would stick to us while we were there.

Occasionally, we attended services at the Baptist church, where we sat with the preacher's son. We knew that at some point in the sermon, the preacher would stop and glare at us. "Are you listening?" he'd ask. "Are you *real-l-l-l-y* listening?" When he stared at us that way, with his slicked-back hair, he looked to me like a falcon.

You probably had heard that we weren't always welcome at the services we attended. At this revival meeting, or that evening prayer service, we might be asked to leave. Usually, it was because one of us laughed. At our own Hood Methodist church, it was always risky to sit behind Mrs. Dodson because if the sermon ran close to noon, the keening of her empty stomach would send us into spasms.

Sometimes, if Bob and I attended a service with several friends, we would just laugh at someone else's laughter, as we did when Bob was stricken at the sight of Fuzzy Jordan's face. Fuzzy sat on the front pew at Hood Methodist church, staring up at Dr. Nelson. His pale blue eyes were rolled upward and his mouth was agape; he seemed awed by the unobstructed view into the preacher's nostrils. Bob's laughing shook our pew and made it creak, which triggered outbreaks of giggling all the way down our row. Dr. Nelson said nothing. He just stopped speaking and pointed silently toward the door of the sanctuary. We knew what he wanted us to do.

Several Sundays after that, Isabel asked Bob and me if we knew anything about the grunting and shoe-scuffing noises that had distracted a number of people during Dr. Nelson's sermon. We both professed to know nothing about such a phenomenon, although I immediately tried to remember if I had grunted or scuffed my shoes as I had clung to the church's brick exterior that morning. Our special Sunday school program had concluded early, and to kill time while you and Isabel were at church, several of us had invented a World War II commando game.

Where the church's brick façade joined the stone foundation, the outcropping of the foundation produced a narrow ledge just wide enough to support a U.S. Army commando in combat boots—provided that the commando could claw a grip in the old building's weathered brick exterior. The ledge was only two feet above the ground, but we pretended that it was at a precipitous height and any attempt to move out upon it would be fraught with danger. Our mission was to mount the ledge at the church entrance and side-step around the entire exterior of the building without falling off.

Negotiating the perimeter of Hood Methodist in this way required considerable effort, and, possibly, that was what the worshippers inside had heard. I didn't confirm any of this with Isabel, however.

You and Isabel let us drive to Billings with Timmy Cowan and his mother one Sunday morning so that we could attend a Roman Catholic mass. The priest performed the mass in Latin, and the whole service was mysterious and inexplicable. From my pew, I studied the carved wood stations of the cross, and heard the priest chant *kyrie eleison, Christe eleison, kyrie eleison* and other strange and beautiful foreign-sounding words that I had never heard before.

I looked around and across the aisle from us, and I saw Wes, the itinerant farm worker that Bob had befriended a week or so earlier. Bob had ascertained two interesting facts about Wes: he was from Iowa, and he preferred raw meat in his hamburgers. So he was something of a curiosity to us, and as I watched Wes kneel with his eyes closed during the mass, I wondered if he missed his family on Sunday mornings. Was he thinking now about his mother and father, his sister, or a girlfriend far away in Iowa? A bell began to ring up front, and each time it rang, Wes slapped the package of cigarettes in his shirt pocket. This deepened the mystery of the strange Catholic rituals. Perhaps they were even more pagan than Mrs. Carson, who led our Protestant vacation Bible school, had said. For a moment, her image came to me, clapping her hands and stamping her foot as she sang "Oh, the B-I-B-L-E … yes, that's the book for me …"

On the drive back to Republic, we asked Tim to show us how to work the rosary beads he was holding. He said he'd do a

"Hail Mary" for us, which he demonstrated in a rapid monotone: "Hail Mary full of grace the Lord is with thee blessed art thou among women and blessed is the fruit of thy womb Jesus. Holy Mary Mother of God pray for us sinners now and at the hour of our death Amen." I then asked Tim why Wes was slapping his cigarette package. Tim laughed, and explained that Wes was just showing his devotion by touching his heart. I liked that.

This ecumenical socializing eventually took us to the First Christian church on Main Street. And that is how we happened to see the Reverend A. Taylor Mahaney saving Gauze Garoutte.

When Reverend Mahaney was new as the pastor of that church, you and Isabel decided to take religion there one Sunday so that you could hear him preach. Bob and I accompanied you, and I think that we must have arrived late because we had to sit in a pew close to the front. From my spot on the pew, the viewing angle was steep, and I couldn't see the new preacher at first. I knew he was there behind the pulpit because I could hear him. I just couldn't see him.

Then, he stepped from behind the pulpit and I got my first look at A. Taylor Mahaney. He was tiny, probably not much over five feet tall. But a wonderful energy sprang from his eyes, and his beaming face resembled the face of a cherub I had seen on a vase in some house we had visited with Isabel.

I didn't listen to much of his sermon, but I couldn't keep my eyes away from his face. It was such a cheerful face, and his eyes were full of life and joy. Bob and I decided to return to hear him again soon. Within a week or so, Bob, who always seemed to know about important events sooner than anyone else, learned that Reverend Mahaney was going to baptize several people. Among them would be Gauze Garoutte, one of our favorite Republic citizens.

Before I go further, Jud, I should explain that if Gauze hadn't been such a popular member of the community and if he hadn't been honored by the school system for his support of Republic's high school athletes, I might never have discovered that we'd been calling him by the wrong nickname. It was years after I'd left Republic, during a summer visit there, that I drove by the new high school's baseball field and saw that it had been named after him. I stared at the sign, which told me that the field had been dedicated to Gose Garoutte. *Gose,* not Gauze. All those years, I'd heard that name and assumed that people were calling him Gauze, the stuff Isabel used to wrap our cuts and scrapes. I never really questioned it, because who could know why adults named things and people the way they did? So, Gauze was the name we used, and, since it still sounds right to me, I'll stick with it (with apologies to Gose).

I remember Gauze as a big, hearty, good-natured man who worked first as the butcher at Eagan's Market and later as the manager of the frozen food locker plant on Main Street. He enjoyed swapping jokes with Bob, and he became a legend of sorts the day a woman drove her car over the curb and crashed through the front of Eagan's Market. According to the legend, after the dust and debris had settled, he strolled calmly from the meat counter to the front of the store and said to the woman, who was unhurt, "Lord, lady, if I'd known you wanted in so bad I'd have opened the front door!"

Now, back to my recollection of the baptism. Bob and I were interested in seeing this ceremony because we Methodists just sprinkled water on our people; at the First Christian church, they dunked theirs in a tank of water. I had witnessed only one dunking previously. One of the country churches near Republic had held a big baptismal service one Sunday in a wide, deep stretch of Terrell Creek. I don't remember how Bob and I happened to be there (I suspect the urge that brought us there had more to do with entertainment than spirituality). But I do remember the preacher who submerged a number of people in Terrell's cold waters. He was a big man with watery blue eyes and a droopy, melancholy face that sloped rapidly from his nose into his neck. When the baptizing was over with, he spoke a prayer in his heavy Ozark twang. His eyes rolled toward heaven, giving him the look of a hound dog begging for scraps; and he said, "Lit's all bow ar hids in a wurd of prar."

Bob and I managed to get good seats in a pew near the front of the First Christian Church sanctuary. As I watched the men fold back the floor panels to reveal the tank of water, I wondered how Reverend Mahaney was going to tilt Gauze back into the water. Gauze was a big man. It would have taken three A. Taylor Mahaneys to make up one Gauze Garoutte. Now, the tiny preacher and Gauze approached the edge of the tank, both of them wearing white robes and looking like Romans. The preacher stepped down into the water and extended his hand to Gauze, who moved carefully down the steps into the baptismal tank.

The two stood together in the water, which was waist-high on Gauze and chest-high on Reverend Mahaney. But the preacher, who looked smaller than ever, put one hand behind Gauze and the other hand on his chest, and began to lower him into the water. Gauze leaned backward and, looking at the ceiling, began to submerge smoothly at first. But then, one of his feet slipped and he fell into the tank, splashing a huge breaker of water toward the front pew. He took the preacher under with him, and they both remained submerged for what seemed to be a long time. I could hear murmuring from the onlookers behind me.

Then, with a mighty spray, Gauze burst upward through the surface of the water. He regained his balance and stood with his eyes squinted, shaking water out of his ears. A moment later, Reverend Mahaney bobbed to the surface behind Gauze and stood up, waving his arms as if he were trying to swim toward the surface.

Water streamed from them both, and they began to grin as they realized that the sound they were hearing was the congregation in an uproar. It was probably the funniest church service ever held in Republic.

Reverend Mahaney looked up at Gauze, and they stood together, laughing. Then the preacher took Gauze's arm and held it high in a sign of victory, and everyone began to applaud.

Things calmed down after Gauze climbed out of the tank, and the baptismal service continued. When the service was over, people spilled out onto the front steps of the church, still laughing at what they had seen. Bob and I felt it had been a very successful visit and one heck of a baptism. And for a change, we hadn't gotten in trouble for laughing in church.

Amen,

Don

Dear Jud:

Ordinarily, one doesn't expect to see a well-dressed businessman and a homeless man chatting over lunch at a fast-food restaurant. They were just at the edge of my vision when I sat down with my lunch and newspaper at a small table near their booth, so I didn't notice them for a few minutes. But something in one man's manner of speaking made me glance at them.

They sat facing each other across the table. The man on the right wore a crisp, white dress shirt and a tie. He had thinning gray-brown hair, and that smooth, bland face that I associate with certain men who work for large corporations. But it was a pleasant face, and he was listening to his booth mate politely and with interest.

The other man—the one whose voice had caused me to look up—wore a red shirt with a button-down collar and epaulets on the shoulders. I noticed that the sleeves were dirty, and as I studied the man more closely, I saw that what he wore was more than just soiled. Both his shirt and pants looked stiffened by layers of dirt that had been ground and pounded in over the weeks since they were last washed. The man's face and hands were wrinkled and darkened by grime and, I guessed, long exposure to the sun and wind. But he had youngish features and his dark, wavy hair was just starting to gray. With better grooming, he would have been handsome.

I wondered why this man, who obviously lived on the streets, was having lunch with a businessman, so I pretended to read my newspaper while I eavesdropped on their conversation.

The homeless man spoke rapidly and nervously in truncated phrases that matched his jerky arm movements. He looked at the top of their table when he spoke and avoided looking at the other man's eyes. He kept reaching for the cigarette package in his shirt pocket, but seemed to change his mind each time. The businessman watched him quietly and nodded sympathetically as his partner spoke about what had been.

I learned that they had attended the same high school. The homeless man, who did most of the talking while I was present, praised his former classmate. I could catch only part of what he said, but I heard fragments such as "... always so good in math ..." and "... heard you were an accountant ..." and "... knew you'd make it."

The businessman smiled and nodded again, and the homeless man related a few things about his own life, most of which I couldn't hear. But the essence of his statement, I gathered, was that he couldn't do much about the way things had turned out and that when things go wrong, you just have to step back and start all over again. And that was what he was doing at this time.

When I got up to leave my table, I glanced at the two men. The homeless man seemed ill at ease, embarrassed, I expect, by the differences between the outcome of his life and that of the businessman. But his old classmate looked at him with a kind, sad expression. One of them had made it; the other had not.

As I drove away, my thoughts about the homeless man led to thoughts about another man we would call homeless today. He had made a place to live across the field from our house in the empty garage behind Bob McClure's old place. You and Isabel called him Mr. Potter, and Bob and I called him the Vegetable Man. In the small garden he had carved out of the adjacent field, he grew vegetables that he peddled to some of the ladies of Republic.

When we asked Isabel why the Vegetable Man lived alone in that old garage, she said it was because he didn't have anyone. After the McClure house had been nearly destroyed by a fire, the house was razed to the stone foundation, and the only part of the property left intact was the small garage building. I never saw the Vegetable Man move in; one day he was just there.

The Vegetable Man must have been one of the dislocated men who came through town on your freight trains during the thirties and early forties. Those who stayed in town for a day or so walked from house to house, asking for a bite to eat. You and Isabel didn't call them homeless people. The name you gave these vagabonds was "bums." But I never got the sense that you were being judgmental. A bum was just a another name for a wanderer.

Bob and I were a little wary of these men. At the sight of one headed our way on Elm Street, we'd scamper into the house and shout, "Mom, a bum's coming down the street!"

She'd usually say, "Well, if he comes to the door, send him to the back porch." When the men knocked on the back door, they were unfailingly polite. They'd take off their hats or caps and ask if she had any work they could do in exchange for some food. She wouldn't give them work, but she always wrapped a bundle of food and handed it to them. They'd nod and thank her kindly and walk on down the street.

Mr. Potter must have liked the looks of Republic, with our quiet, shady streets. Perhaps he was just weary of traveling, or ill. For whatever reason, he made the garage next door to us his home, and he was part of our existence for a short time.

When Bob or I saw him coming up the front walk, we'd run to the kitchen and say, "Mom, the Vegetable Man is here!" Then we'd walk to the front door with her to greet him. He would stand on the top step of our front porch, smile, and extend his big wicker basket. It would be full of tomatoes, onions, potatoes, lettuce, green beans, and parsnips. If I stood close enough, I could catch the sharp, fresh plant smells mingled with the smell of black, moist earth. The odor made me think of the evening you dug up that huge potato in our World War II Victory Garden. You lifted the massive clump of rich soil to show me the potato, and the cool, dark soil gave off a wild, pleasant fragrance that filled my nostrils.

The Vegetable Man smelled good, too. It was a composite odor of gardens, tobacco juice, bonfire smoke, and clothes that needed washing. He seemed gentle and shy, and I liked him, although he seldom spoke to us. On my way to Leland Brown's house one morning, I passed by the Vegetable Man's garage house, and I saw him working in his garden. He moved slowly, cultivating the soil along a row of tomato plants. The hoe he was using looked ancient, and the blade kept falling off the end of the handle. He'd stoop to retrieve the blade and patiently tap it back onto the handle. When he noticed that I was watching him, he smiled and plucked a plump red tomato from a vine, dusted it off on his sleeve, and handed it to me. "Eat this with a little salt," he said. "They're best when they're right fresh from the vine." I took it home and washed it thoroughly at the kitchen sink, because I was afraid of catching germs. But the Vegetable Man was right. I sat on the back steps with a salt shaker and ate the tomato. It was delicious.

Sometimes I stood in our front yard and watched him going from house to house with his basket of vegetables. At each house, he knocked on the door and then stepped back to wait. When someone answered the door, he touched the brim of his black felt hat and bowed slightly, then lifted the basket to show all the vegetables it contained. When he spoke, he held his head down, timidly glancing up now and then from under the brim of his hat.

If he didn't make a sale, he touched the hat brim, turned, and shuffled slowly to the next house. Isabel usually bought something from him, although you grew all the vegetables we could eat. The Vegetable Man's tomatoes and potatoes especially, she said, seemed bigger and nicer than ours. I don't believe she really thought his vegetables were better than yours. This was probably her justification for giving him some money. I could tell she genuinely liked him, and she called him a "nice, lonely old man."

The Vegetable Man became such a familiar figure on our street that I was deeply affected when you brought news that he had died. I had seen people at his garage house, and I thought he might be sick when I saw Uncle Bob Thurman's black hearse, which was sometimes used as an ambulance, backed up to the garage door.

Several days after they took him away, Bob and I went over to the Vegetable Man's place. The door wasn't locked, so we went in. He had tried to make it as homey as he could. A rocking chair sat on the concrete floor, and next to it was a table covered with a red-and-white checkered oilcloth. On his small bed was a ragged patchwork quilt, rumpled from where it had been pulled back. There was still a depression in the thin mattress, I knew, from where the Vegetable Man's body had lain.

He had nailed flattened cardboard boxes to the exposed studs of the garage's interior, giving the walls a more finished look. Where the boxes overlapped, parts of words were hidden. I looked around, and read *Super Sud-*, *Toilet Pa-,* and *Canned Green Be-*. What was left of his last meal was on a small, cold kerosene stove. A saucepan contained some molding boiled potatoes, and a skillet was half-filled with congealed gravy that had begun to crack. After a few days, someone came and moved all of the Vegetable Man's things out.

Sometimes, on our way home from school, we stopped and looked into the empty garage house. It was gloomy inside, and the leaves that had drifted through the open door made the place seem even emptier and lonelier. My stomach always felt funny when we went inside, so I never stayed long. It wasn't fear I felt, but rather a hollow, sweet sadness.

The days took us through autumn, then winter and spring. By the time school was out again for summer vacation, our memory of the Vegetable Man had receded. It was hard to think that anyone had ever lived in the old garage with its doors always open and the grass and weeds so high.

That was the summer we used the garage in our war games. One afternoon, we pretended that German soldiers had occupied the building. Our squad's mission was to drive them out, and we attacked the garage with rocks and green walnuts.

I can still hear the bright, brittle crashing noises we caused as our missiles broke out the glass windows. And I still feel a little ashamed when I recall our laughter and the way we treated the gentle, lonely Vegetable Man's little house.

Don

> *Love came down at Christmas, love all lovely, love divine ...*
> Christina Rossetti
> Hymn 84, Episcopal Hymnal 1982

Dear Jud:

This old Christmas carol isn't as well-known or often-sung as others that are so familiar. But the homely grace of the carol's first line appeals strongly to me, and it expresses a sentiment that I didn't feel until late on the day before Christmas in 1944.

That Christmas Eve began as a dull gray day in Republic. The sky was battleship-colored, and even the snow covering our yard was dingy—tainted by soot that fell from the coal smoke billowing from chimneys along Elm Street. I felt melancholy, due mostly to the war news. The feeling was intensified by the drab scene outside when I looked out our dining room window. It seemed that we wouldn't be having our usual, joyous family gathering. Things were going to be different this year.

Bob was outside on some errand. Patty was in the kitchen helping Isabel prepare some desserts for our Christmas dinner. Phyllis, who had joined the U.S. Navy Nurse Corps, was in Springfield, working at St. John's Hospital while awaiting her orders to report to the naval hospital at Great Lakes, Illinois. That's where, in only a few months, she would meet George, who had been injured when his Navy bi-wing Stearman training aircraft crashed. Jean and baby Ann had come home to stay with us for a few months. She and Malcolm had been married shortly before he was sent to Britain to take part in the D-Day landings at Normandy. Now, Malc was a second lieutenant with the U.S. Army Medical Corps and was leading an ambulance company somewhere in Belgium—although we didn't yet know that. Malc would miss the next month's celebration of his daughter Ann's first birthday.

The morning's radio news had carried reports of the fighting in the Ardennes region in France and Belgium. During the past week, the German army's surprise offensive had broken through American lines. We worried that Malc's unit might be involved in the fighting, which the newscasters were calling the "Battle of the Bulge." If we had known how close he was to the snowy, forested area where the German counterattack began, we'd have worried even more.

I wandered into the living room and turned on the radio by your green chair. One of the stations was broadcasting a program of carols, and as I listened to "There's a Song in the Air" ("There's a star in the sky ..."), I thought of the Christmas pageant at Hood Methodist church several years earlier. Our Sunday school class sang that carol and "Silent Night." After we performed, there was a commotion in the back of the church, and Sam Hock, dressed as Santa Claus, came down the aisle handing out big mesh bags full of oranges, ribbon candy, English walnuts, and gigantic candy canes. I was at that awkward stage of still wanting to believe in Santa but wondering about the rumors I'd heard. And even though I knew this elf was Sam, I was still awed, because those magical bags of fruit and candy, his bushy beard, and the red-and-white costume all seemed to carry the full authority of Santa.

By five o'clock, the winter sky was darkening, and I decided to walk downtown to help you close your office. You'd been keeping especially long hours for the past three years. The war touched everyone, even people who lived in a small town in the Missouri Ozarks.

It was cozy inside the old depot office as I stood by the warm stove and watched you wind things up for the evening. The Western Union telegraph receivers had been clattering, and you'd typed several telegraph messages. Outside, the snow was starting again.

You shoved the telegrams into your overcoat pocket and asked if I wanted to help deliver them. I did, and I bundled into my mackinaw and galoshes while you banked the coals in the potbelly stove. As you locked the door to the inner office, I stood in the dark waiting room. I looked out one of the windows and could see the bright parallel lines of the main line tracks against the snow.

We left the depot and crunched across the snowy gravel toward the downtown district. Warm lights from the store windows reflected on the wet sidewalks as we walked through town. A cardboard Santa Claus face beamed at us from the bourbon display inside Juggy's Place. In the back of the liquor store, I saw Juggy Snyder just standing there, probably wanting to close up but hoping to make one more Christmas Eve sale.

It was snowing heavily by the time we walked away from the lights of the business district and entered the residential blocks of North Main Street. I watched snowflakes falling through the glow from a streetlight, and when you stopped to deliver the first of the telegrams, I stood on the sidewalk and waited. Over the past several years, you'd had to deliver a number of telegrams that began with "We regret to inform you ..." Isabel told us once that she could tell by the look on your face when you'd had to make one of those deliveries. But tonight, these were Christmas messages—happy telegrams you didn't mind delivering. And as I waited in the snow and stillness of the night, I began to feel some of the old magic of Christmas Eve.

We walked quietly along a side street to the next home and then headed back to Elm Street where you delivered the last telegram. Neither of us said anything as we walked toward home. I listened to the squiffing sound my galoshes made in the snow, and I felt the wet, cold touch of snowflakes against my face.

We reached the lot adjacent to our house, and you said, "Look at that! Isabel's got the whole place looking like an ornament!" I'd never seen our house the way it looked that night. Every light inside was blazing. The Christmas tree was shining in the living room window, and the porch light cast a glow across the rippled, snowy surface of the front yard.

Isabel and Pat had been busy baking and that fragrance seemed to warm the cold night air. When I took off my galoshes and left them on the porch, I left the dreariness I'd felt earlier outside, too.

Just before bedtime, some carolers came and we stood on the porch listening to "Hark! The Herald Angel Sing," "O Little Town of Bethlehem," and "We Three Kings." We applauded the carolers, and they moved across the snow to the Cantrells' house and then to the Fugitts'.

Isabel said we'd all get chilled, so the rest of you went inside. But I stayed on the porch, breathing the cold, pure air. The carolers were far down the street, and I could hear them faintly singing "There's a Song in the Air." I stood there, shivering, listening to them until their voices were too faint to hear, because it was Christmas Eve, and I didn't want the wonder of it to end.

Don

Dear Jud:

Nearly always, by the time evening rolled around, Bob and I were out of your green chair—to which we were often banished for misbehavior—and you were in it. After supper, after your garden or furnace chores, it was time for you to lean back in your beloved green chair, raise the foot rest, light your pipe, snap on the radio. and settle in for a pleasant hour or so with the light classics and operetta music. I often sat cross-legged on the floor beside your chair with my drawing paper or a Tinker Toy project, and that is where I learned to love music.

Absorbed as I was in my projects, I wasn't consciously listening to your radio shows. But as your Philco radio poured out music of the *Bell Telephone Hour,* the *Firestone Hour,* and the *Hour of Charm* with Phil Spitalni and his all-girl orchestra, a current of notes flowed like a melodic brook over the arm of your chair and into my ears below. I heard performances by Nelson Eddy, Jeanette MacDonald, Gladys Swarthout, Thomas L. Thomas, and Evelyn and Her Magic Violin. And my feelings for music began to grow.

But I wasn't aware that this was happening until the night I envisioned myself playing a musical instrument. That happened in 1942 at one of the summer outdoor community band concerts at the Republic band shell. Of the many band concerts we attended during those war years, that one stands apart. That one inspired me. I was only eight years old, but that night, as I sat in the darkness, listening, I felt a kinship with those band members. And I could hardly wait to be one of them.

Bob and I sat on the first row of the benches in front of the band. These were our favorite seats, because we had an unobstructed view of the band director, Bud Thurman. Bud stood at the front of the stage waving his arms at the band, which was made up of current and former high-school band members—the men dressed in slacks and short-sleeve shirts and the women in the cotton summer dresses that were fashionable in the forties. You and Isabel sat somewhere behind us on the rough plank seats.

The band proceeded thrillingly toward the end of some overture—one of those pieces in which the finale consists of a series of heroic chords separated by dramatic pauses. Bud's arms were pumping up and down as he led the band through a thicket of notes and, with a chopping motion, elicited the first of the final chords. The musicians observed just the briefest silence—during which Bob began to applaud. Then, another up-and-down stroke of Bud's arms produced another crashing chord, followed by another pause, which was punctuated by Bob's lonely applause. There came still another chord and pause, and Bob began to clap again. But this time, Bud, who was still holding his arms high in the air, turned his head toward us and shouted, "We'll be through in a minute, boy!"

Bud brought his arms down one last time and the band responded with a long chord which faded into silence. Bob waited this time until he heard others in the audience whistling and applauding; then we both joined in. Bud stood with his arms at his side and bowed, and when he raised his head, he glared sternly at Bob. Then he winked an eye and grinned.

My mind was full as we walked along Main Street after the concert. I wondered why summer air smells different at night, especially the air this night. It was a blend of your pipe smoke, auto exhaust, and café aromas. I thought about the unusual day we had spent together. It all seemed somehow connected and significant, although, of course, those big words weren't going through my head at that moment.

That Saturday had begun with a morning trip to Bennett Brothers Barber Shop. You sat with us in the row of chairs against the wall, and we took turns looking at war pictures in *Life* magazine while we awaited our turns. At eight years of age,

Bob and I were still too small to sit on the leather seats of the big, high-backed barber chairs. So Claude Bennett and Shrimp, his brother, placed boards across the arms of their chairs to form improvised seating that would elevate Bob and me enough for the barbers to reach our heads with their scissors and combs. When it was my turn, I would usually climb into Claude's chair and sit on the board, trying to avoid the gazes of the row of customers and loafers that sat against the wall facing me. While Claude cut my hair, I picked out things to stare at. I was fascinated by the ornate cast iron foot-rest, which bore the word KOKEN embossed in block letters. I was becoming a fairly proficient reader, so I was able to pronounce the word, but I didn't know what it meant. And I was too shy to ask Claude. If I had, he'd probably have said "Oh, that's the name of the outfit that makes these chairs."

Bob preferred to have his hair cut by Shrimp Bennett. We always argued about which of the brothers was the better barber, Claude or Shrimp. The brothers seldom spoke to each other, which I thought was odd. When Shrimp moved out several years later and opened his own barbershop down the street next to the post office, Bob began to get his haircuts at the new shop. I stayed with Claude.

The end of our haircuts was marked by a ritual we loved. Claude would unhook the cloth that he had pinned around my neck, brush away the loose hair cuttings, turn my chair toward the mirror, and point toward the row of hair oil bottles that sat on a small shelf. There were bottles of Bay Rum, Rose Hair Oil, Jeris Hair Tonic, and Wildroot Crème Oil. After I'd had a few seconds to survey the bottles, Claude would ask, "What'll it be today, Don? Polecat Piss [the Jeris] or Buzzard's Puke [the Crème Oil]?" Bob and I always monitored each other's choices because we would never wear the same hair oil. If I selected Buzzard's Puke, Bob was sure to request Polecat Piss.

After you paid Claude and Shrimp 25 cents each for our haircuts, we would follow you out the door and on toward the Farmer's Exchange, several doors away. Walking behind Bob, I could smell Polecat Piss, and I wondered if my own new-cut hair, anointed with Buzzard's Puke, was as fragrant. At the Farmer's Exchange, we would watch you buy two chickens for Sunday dinner. On our way home, we'd take the back way, across the tracks by the section gang's shack, along Harrison Street to Maple Avenue, and then to Elm. You carried the chickens, which squawked occasionally inside the burlap bag, because you said we weren't yet tall enough to handle them.

After lunch that Saturday, Bob and I spent the afternoon playing war games with some friends. When evening came, Isabel joined us for the walk back to town and to the small park where the bandstand was located. Bill Hood, Sam Hock, and other members of your lodge were cooking hot dogs on the big stone barbecue pit in the park. Isabel had decided that we'd eat our supper there. Bob and I each selected two of the plump, sizzling hot dogs (which, on that night and in that setting, became "Eine Kleine Knackwurst"). Isabel placed them in buns, slathered mustard and ketchup over them, and heaped potato chips onto our plates. We pulled cold bottles of root beer from the ice-filled soft-drink chest and then found a bench away from the smoky grill to enjoy our supper.

Daylight was fading by the time we had finished our hot dogs, and street lights and store lights were coming on as we strolled back to Main Street. Most of the businesses along the two-block business district stayed open late on Saturdays. For the farm families who lived in the rural areas surrounding Republic, Saturdays were market days. They came to town to purchase goods and supplies, do a little socializing, and, of course, to attend the band concert.

Downtown Republic was transformed on Saturday nights. The store fronts and windows glittered with lights, people crowded along the sidewalks, Main Street was filled with the sound and smells of traffic, and diagonally parked vehicles lined both sides of the street.

Someone who knew something about sound systems had mounted speakers on the corner of the Owen and Short Hardware store and had strung a wire all the way down Grant Street to the band park. The sound of band music on Main Street contributed to the festival atmosphere in the downtown area. As we approached the speakers, I could hear the sounds of band members warming up, and Isabel said we'd better go find good places to sit. Bob and I left you and ran back to the park to claim our spots on the front bench.

The Saturday night concert program always began with lively marching music. Even without the speakers on Main Street, the downtown blocks resounded to "Thunder and Blazes," "Washington Post," "National Emblem," "High School Cadets," "Our Director," and, always, "Stars and Stripes Forever." America was at war, and the first notes of this classic march always brought us all to our feet. When Joe Connell came home on furlough from the U.S. Marines, Bud Thurman featured him in a tribute to the Marine Corps. Joe, who'd been a percussionist with the high school band, stood at center stage in his crisp red, white, and blue Marine dress uniform, rattling his snare drum while the band played "Semper Fideles." I don't remember whether Joe experienced combat during the war, but I do know he was a hero that night.

At intermission, band members drank cool drinks (in a few instances spiked with bourbon) and mingled with the audience. Then the second half of the concert began. This half usually featured favorite overtures and light classics. When Bob and I later began to play at the Saturday night concerts, much of the music was familiar to us since it included compositions our high school band had performed at the state music festival and other concerts: the *William Tell Overture, Malaguena,* the *Oberon Overture, Die Fledermaus,* the *Grand Canyon Suite,* the *Morning, Noon and Night Overture,* the *Peer Gynt Suite,* the *Gayne Ballet Suite* ("Saber Dance" was the audience favorite from this suite), *Turkish Dance,* and the *Light Cavalry Overture.* Bud also threw in such crowd pleasers as "American Patrol," "The Continental," "Bolero," "Whistler and His Dog," "The Bugler's Holiday," "Jealousy," "Pavane," and "The Teddy Bears' Picnic."

After Bob and I joined the Republic High School band, we knew that we could count on seeing you and Isabel at every concert and performance. It meant a great deal to both of us, although we never told you how much we valued that support. The band qualified to go to the state music festival every year Bob and I were members of the band, and I guess you and Isabel were just as proud of that as we were.

At one of those state music festivals, which were always held at the University of Missouri in Columbia, I visited one of the solo competition rooms and listened to a cornet player perform a piece called "My Silver Horn." The melody of this Civil War era composition was hauntingly beautiful, and the performer was a tall, athletic-looking boy who was greatly admired by all the girls. After that experience, I dreamed that someday I would perform that piece at one of the Saturday night concerts, and that girls would give me the worshipful gazes he received. Alas, I could never find the sheet music for "My Silver Horn."

Jud, I'm glad that you and Isabel weren't at one performance. Instead of distinguishing myself, I embarrassed myself, and the two of you might have been embarrassed for me— although, come to think of it, you'd have probably seen the humor in the situation. Our band traveled to Joplin, Missouri, to perform a concert at Joplin Senior High School. The program included a number called "The Three Jacks," which was a trumpet trio featuring Gary Baumberger, Robert Thurman, and me.

During the number the band performed prior to our trio, I was balancing my trumpet on my knee. The trumpet slipped and fell to the stage floor, landing on the bell of the horn. It hit the floor like a toilet plunger. When I picked up my instrument, the thin metal of the bell on that inexpensive Getzen trumpet had curled back and it looked like a stepped-on morning glory. Bud's all-seeing eyes had witnessed the incident, and he gave me a sharp look as he held the band on the final note of the piece. It was now time for us to stand at the front of the stage and perform. There was nothing I could do but face the music—and the crowd. The band played the introduction to the trio, and, as we brought our trumpets to our lips to play, I could hear snickering. I glanced at the front rows of the audience. It seemed that every eye was fixed on the crumpled bell of my trumpet and every face was smirking. My own face felt hot but the accident apparently hadn't affected the tone of my trumpet, and we received loud applause at the end of our number.

It has been many years since that Saturday night band concert I described earlier, so I can't recall which musical selection aroused Billy Burris, who was spending the evening in the Republic jailhouse. As I remember it, the town lockup looked like one of those squat, concrete German bunkers shown in newsreels of the D-Day invasion. The jail was located just a few yards behind the bandstand, and was also conveniently near the back door of Juggy Snyder's beer joint and pool hall—which is where Billy had been prior to being escorted to the jail.

Billy was famous for being annoying. Just looking at him annoyed most people. He was a scrawny little man with a hunchback. He wore shirts that were too large, and pants that were too short. He never tied his shoes, which looked too big and clumped irritatingly as he hobbled around the pool hall. Those traits alone would have made Billy unpopular among Juggy's patrons, but he also was overly fond of onions, never bathed, and became sarcastic and pugnacious after a few beers. These habits often led to his expulsion from the pool hall, especially after Wib Gibbs became the manager.

I was walking on the sidewalk near Juggy's Place one morning when the screen door banged open and Billy came tumbling out. Then Wib's face thrust from the doorway, and, while Billy skittered over the curb and into the street, Wib shouted, "Stay outa here, you God Blessed oh-rang yew-tang! And don't come back no more today!"

As I said, I don't remember which piece inspired Billy during that Saturday night's concert, but it must have been one of the overtures. Bud was conducting the band through the number when I noticed a jarring sound, as if there had been a terrible accident in the percussion section. It was a rhythmic, metallic clanging.

After a few seconds, I realized the noise was coming from out of the darkness. When the music rose to a crescendo, I no longer heard the banging. But a diminuendo followed, and over the hushed music came the rhythmic clanging again. A man behind us laughed and whispered "Sounds like somebody—probably old Billy—is trying to join the band."

Bob and I left our seats and moved to the barbecue grill, where we could see the jail. And the man was right. Someone inside was banging something against the jail's steel door. Each time he struck the door, sparks flew through the ventilation holes. Smoky Smith, who was watching and chuckling, told us that the occupant was indeed Billy. We later heard that he had torn the leg off the jail stove and used it as a mallet.

Bud wasn't amused by Billy's improvisations. When the band changed from four-four time to three-four, Billy, listening closely, altered his beat. And when the music returned to four-four time, Billy quickly adjusted his beat to conform with the band's tempo. His accompaniment continued throughout the number and ended only a couple of beats after the band finished. Bud gamely smiled back at the laughing audience, and bowed in thanks to the applause.

I found you and Isabel in the crowd, and you were laughing, too, as Bud walked to the edge of the platform. He turned toward the jailhouse and, in the manner of symphony conductors who direct applause to orchestra members, he bowed and gestured into the darkness toward the jailhouse. The audience appreciated this, and so did the band members, and soon everyone rose to give Billy a standing ovation.

After the concert, you and Isabel allowed Bob and me to play for a while with our friends, dashing around and wrestling in the little park. Even as I played in the balmy darkness, I was thinking about the members of the band—how they sat in the bright lights on the high stage and the way they obeyed Bud Thurman's waving arms to produce such magical music.

Lying in bed that night, I imagined that I was a trumpet player with the band, and I wondered what Billy Burris's thoughts were as he lay on his jailhouse cot. And now, all these years later, I wonder if Billy, lying there in his dark little dungeon, was pleased that he'd finally done something that people applauded.

Don

Dear Jud:

I could never tell you how much I hated the railroad job you arranged for me.

Railroading was your life, and it was to that steady work that all seven of us owed our full bellies during the thirties. Although you never spoke to us directly about it, you may have hoped that either Bob or I (even both of us) would have careers with the Frisco—perhaps, like you, as a depot agent. Bob had enlisted in the U.S. Army after high school, so when you heard that the depot agent in Bolivar, Missouri, was looking for a station helper, you saw a possible career opportunity for me there. You believed that a depot would be a good place to begin a life's journey. But that depot just wasn't the right place for me to begin mine.

It must have been obvious to you and Isabel that I was floundering after I graduated from high school. And it must have bothered you to see me fail at my first full-time job—washing cars at Montgomery Buick in Springfield. Washing cars for eight hours a day wasn't that difficult. And I washed them with such care that the make-ready supervisor said he'd never seen such clean cars. It was just that he wasn't seeing a sufficient number of them coming out of the car-washing bay. I needed to wash cars less thoroughly and wash more of them, he said.

And so I tried. But I believe my days were numbered even if there hadn't been Black Tuesday. In that one day, I: nearly ruined the fabric top of Mr. Montgomery's personal convertible; washed a showroom-bound sedan with its windows open, soaking the upholstery; and backed a pickup truck into the side of a new car about to be delivered to the customer.

At supper that night, I was glum. You and Isabel both stared into your plates as I related what I had done that day. But then you said you had some news that I might be glad to hear, and you told me about the station helper job in Bolivar. I had never cared much for the projects you had assigned to Bob and me at your depot. But, at that moment, painting a rhinoceros would have seemed attractive compared with facing the people at Montgomery Buick again. You suggested that I go back in the morning and tell them I had taken another job.

Cheered by the thought that I would have to put in only another day or so as a car washer, I returned to Montgomery Buick the next morning and gave my supervisor the news. Things went better than I had expected. He congratulated me heartily, took me to the business office, obtained a check for the few days they owed me, and sent me on my way with his best wishes for a successful railroad career.

This left me the rest of the week to think about the new job, which was mine for the taking because you had made, as they say, the necessary arrangements. At first, I felt some excitement about going to Bolivar. A few years earlier, something extraordinary had happened to me there: I had, in a way, met the President of the United States. I would think more about that thrilling moment during the lonely days that were to come.

You and the Frisco agent there had hammered out the details of my budding railroad career. I would work Monday through Friday at the depot, live in a hotel several blocks away during the week, and return home by bus on weekends. My duties would include typing and other routine paper work, sweeping the office and freight room, and helping load and unload Frisco freight trucks.

On the Sunday before I reported for work, I said goodbye to you and Isabel and caught the Ozark Trailways bus to Springfield, where I'd board another bus and ride the thirty-two miles to Bolivar. Before we were two miles out of Republic, something happened that I didn't at first recognize as a bad sign, an omen of ill things to come in Bolivar: A young boy's voice caused me to turn in my seat and look behind me. He and a fifty-ish woman I took to be his grandmother were seated in the row behind mine, and he was singing, "Me and my grandma are going to town" in a whiny voice.

Then he began a maddening series of variations in which he began each word with the same consonant, as in, "Te tand ty tanma tar toing to town. Pee pand py panma par poing poo pown. Kee kand ky kanma kar koing ku kown. Zee zand zy zanma zar zoing zoo zown." Et cetera. He went on and on until, by my reckoning, he had used all but two consonants of the alphabet. I heard grandma quietly advise him not to try the letters Q and X.

After some minutes of this, I turned and glared at the boy. Grandma, who was vigilant and saw me, glared back. The boy, sure of her continued approval and protection, became bolder and brattier and sang his variations until we had nearly reached the bus station in Springfield. When the bus stopped, the passengers moved into the aisle and began to shuffle to the front. I'd been slow to get out of my seat, so the boy and his grandmother were in line ahead of me. He turned to give me an impudent look. I responded by making a monster face at him, which I held until I glanced toward the bus driver. He was watching me in his rearview mirror. I quickly contorted my face into various expressions, slapping at it as if some invisible bug were bedeviling me. I didn't look at the driver as I stepped off the bus, located my suitcase and headed for the terminal.

My bus ride from Springfield to Bolivar was without incident. We drove north on Highway 13 and reached Bolivar in about an hour. I walked from the town's dingy bus station to my hotel, which was in the center of town, near the Polk County courthouse. The lobby was as quiet as a tomb when I entered, except for the squeaking of pants against leatherette when two elderly men pivoted in their chairs to study me, a stranger in town. I registered at the small desk, breathing the mildew/bar soap smell that pervaded the lobby, then walked up a flight of stairs to my room. The walls of the room were painted pale blue, and the bed was covered by a limp chenille bedspread, also pale blue.

The air in the room was close and carried undertones of that same mildew-and-bar-soap odor, so I raised a window that looked upon the town square. The air that came in smelled like summer afternoon, and it brought to mind the quotation from Henry James that I had read in Mildred Heagerty's English class during my senior year:

> *Summer afternoon—summer afternoon; to me those have always been the two most beautiful words in the English language.*

I began to wish that I was sitting on our front porch on shady Elm Street. Being in this room, in this town, made me feel lonely, so I unpacked the few things I'd brought and left the hotel. I saw a restaurant across the square, and I thought a good meal might cheer me up. A pretty waitress with long blonde hair recommended their hamburger and homemade french fries. The meal was delicious, and when the same waitress smiled at me while taking my money at the cash register, I briefly fantasized that she might be wondering, "Who is this handsome stranger?"

The thought of going back to the hotel depressed me, so I decided to take a look at the town. The streets were silent on this Sunday afternoon. I walked around the square, which was dominated by the courthouse building, and I passed stores and businesses with small-town names: Braithwait's, Hacker's, Hutcheson & Company. I spotted the Drake Theater, where I would pass a number of lonely evenings watching movies.

I decided to try to find the Frisco depot so that I'd know how to get there in the morning. But when I stopped at the hotel to ask the desk clerk for directions, she told me that it was right on West Broadway, which was just around the corner, and that it would take me only ten or fifteen minutes to walk there in the morning. That was when I decided to try to locate the exact spot on that quiet residential street where, five years earlier, I had come face-to-face with the president of the United States, Harry S Truman.

I remembered approximately where that had occurred, and, after wandering up and down several streets, I found what appeared to be the location I was looking for. It was in the center of the block and the trees looked familiar. I stepped off the curb into the street, just as I had done on that July day in 1948; looked to the right up the street; and tried to re-create the moment that I saw the president's car coming toward me.

Bob and I were eighth-graders in 1948, but Bud Thurman had let us start playing in the Republic High School band. That summer, the band had been invited to participate in a parade and ceremonies in Bolivar to dedicate a new memorial statue placed there to honor Simón Bolívar, the emancipator of Venezuela. When Harry Truman was still a senator from Missouri, the Venezuelan ambassador had contacted him and said that if his state had a town named after Simón Bolíivar, Venezuela would be glad to place a statue of the great liberator there.

Word of that offer soon got around to the citizens in eight or nine other towns in the United States named Bolivar. And when the people of Bolivar, New York, heard that the Venezuelans had offered the statue to our Bolivar instead of theirs, they were "hurt, mad, and sad," according to the editor of that town's newspaper. Furthermore, he huffed, addressing the residents of our Bolivar, "We are as much a 'city' as you are."

Actually, in terms of size, they weren't. The population of Bolivar, Missouri, in 1948 was 2,636, compared with the eastern version's population of an even 2,000. F. L. Stufflebam, editor of the Missouri town's newspaper, answered the New York editor with a double-edged reply, saying that "Bolivar, New York, should grow a little." And then, in the spirit of the feisty president who was headed for town, Stufflebam added that "Bolivar, Missouri, is the best town anywhere for its size!"

So that is how the statue of Simón Bolívar came to be erected four blocks south of the county courthouse in Bolivar and dedicated on the day after the Fourth of July in 1948. While I watched, Venezuela's president, Romulo Gallegos, presented the statue, and our president, Harry S Truman, accepted on behalf of the people of Bolivar *and* the United States.

Isabel had had to do some alterations on my band uniform before we made the trip. I was thin and the uniform was too large. I remember wearing pajama pants under the trousers, because the heavy wool fabric was intolerably itchy in the hot July weather.

We rode to Bolivar in school buses early that Monday morning and were assembling for the parade through town by 9 AM, about the time the presidential train was due to arrive at the depot. I noticed that the fire department had hosed down the asphalt all along the parade route, perhaps to impress the two leaders as well as the hordes of visitors. Everywhere I looked, I saw people rushing and talking excitedly. At one point, I heard two men kidding each other about competing in two of the festive day's events: a fat man's race and a cracker-eating contest.

Our band and a couple of other high school bands practiced playing the "Star Spangled Banner" with the U.S. Air Force Band. Shortly after that, we marched to our assigned location and the parade began. People cheered loudly as we marched through the town square. But not everyone in Bolivar cared that history was being made. As we marched past the photographers' bleachers, I glanced at the pool hall behind the bleachers. Inside, half a dozen patrons were shooting pool, oblivious to the commotion of the parade.

At some point as we marched along Bolivar's streets, I lost the mouthpiece of my trumpet. It must have dropped out while I was holding the instrument in marching position. I didn't notice that it was missing until the parade was over.

Since we were to be part of a mass band performance of the American and Venezuelan national anthems at the site of the statue, I had to borrow a mouthpiece from another trumpet player. I didn't like putting my lips against someone else's mouthpiece, and I kept feeling the urge to spit. But that concern left me when Bud Thurman brought us to attention. I felt nervous, but important. We were about to accompany a famous opera singer, Gladys Swarthout, as she sang the two anthems. Bud told us to play our best because she also had been born in Missouri. I watched her sing while I played my third-trumpet part, and thought that Jean, who so loved to listen to radio broadcasts of the opera on Saturday afternoons, would be proud that her twin brothers were accompanying the famous operatic star.

We were close to the speakers' platform, and I could see the honored guests all standing at attention. I found it hard to believe that I was staring at the heads, literally, of two different nations at the same time. President Gallegos came to the microphone and presented the statue not to just the people of Bolivar, but to all citizens of the United States. President Truman was tanned and fit-looking in his light-colored suit and fedora. He accepted the statue for the city and the nation and made a short speech. I didn't follow his speech carefully except for the part in which he said that it was a special honor for this city in his home state. The president's remarks were followed by a benediction, and the dedication ceremonies ended.

We marched back to the parking area at Bolivar's high school and put our instruments in the buses. We weren't scheduled to leave for a while so I decided to retrace the parade route and look for my mouthpiece. I walked the route with my head down, sweeping my eyes back and forth across the pavement. I'd walked through several business blocks and was on a shady residential block when I heard a commotion.

I looked to my right and saw, coming toward me at a leisurely speed, a long, black convertible. As it approached, I could see that it was being driven by a man in uniform. Two men were riding in the rear seat, and one of them was wearing a light-colored suit and fedora. The convertible drew very close, and I recognized the

119

man in the hat. It was President Truman, and he was going to pass within feet of me.

I quickly stepped to the curb of the street, wondering what to do. I wondered if Secret Service men would be suspicious of me. I wondered if I should salute, since I was wearing a uniform. But no, I couldn't salute, because I wasn't wearing my band cap. So I decided to stand rigidly at attention.

Women's voices were coming from somewhere, and I could hear the sound of the engine as the shiny, black convertible drove by. Standing at the curb, not moving a muscle, arms clamped to my sides, I swiveled my eyes and looked into President Truman's face, now only a yard or two away. Our eyes met for an instant, and he might have been thinking, "What an odd young man." Then his face stiffened slightly, and he said something to the driver. The car picked up speed and drove on down the street.

Then I saw what must have prompted the president to request more speed: Three middle-aged women were running behind the president's convertible, wobbling on their high heels, waving white handkerchiefs over their heads, and crying, "Harry? Harry!"

I watched Harry Truman's car speed to the end of the block, turn right, and drive away, probably toward the presidential train at the depot. Realizing that they had been driven-away-from, the women stopped running and stood in the middle of the street for a moment, panting and talking excitedly. Then, they walked on, never noticing me, and I resumed my search for the mouthpiece. I never found it.

And now, standing at the same curb again, I thought about that thrilling Monday in 1948, and I wondered what the Monday that was coming tomorrow would be like.

It wasn't what you and I had hoped it might be. The depot agent didn't like me. I could tell immediately. During the weeks that followed, I struggled with the job, never seeming to please him. I validated his negative feelings for me when I misplaced a manifest that identified a string of boxcars that were part of an arriving freight train. While the engine sat on the tracks, chugging impatiently, the agent and train crew frantically tried to determine which cars needed to be uncoupled and left in Bolivar. And when I finally remembered where I had put the manifest and produced it, they showed no gratitude.

Fate kindly intervened again when Neal Gray, your friend from Ozark, called you to tell you about an opening for a clerk at the Union National Bank in Springfield. When you mentioned it to me during my next weekend at home, I eagerly said that I wanted the job. I could see some disappointment in your eyes, but you knew that I was miserable in Bolivar, and you sensed that I wasn't meant to pursue a railroad career. (I also suspect that the crusty old agent in Bolivar had called you to complain about me.)

I returned to Republic and began the bank job at which I worked happily until it was time to serve my two years of active duty with the U.S. Naval Reserve.

And I did get to march for President Truman another time. I don't remember the occasion, but the president came to Springfield to review a parade in which my Naval Reserve unit participated. As we marched past the reviewing stand, I obeyed the "Eyes Right!" command and looked toward the president, who stood holding his hat over his heart.

Once again, I looked into the face of President Truman and it seemed that he looked back at me. As I recall that moment, I visualize a cartoon dialogue balloon over the president's head, and inside, the words, "Why, there's that odd young man I saw in Bolivar!"

I'm sorry that my railroad career didn't go anywhere and that you were never able to brag about your son, the banker. But, at least, you *were* able to say that your son had met the president of the United States, in a way.

Don

Woody Blossoms

Dear Jud:

I was thirteen years old when Republic discovered that Woody Kettel had changed. I was unaware of many things at that age, but when I saw what I saw, even I knew there was something very different about Woody. It was early in the morning and I was on my way to the post office. As I walked past the photo studio on Main Street, I glanced at the window and saw that the photographer had put a new portrait on display. It was a studio photo of an elderly man wearing a tall-crowned cowboy hat and elaborately ornamented, Roy Rogers–style shirt and trousers. He was sighting down the barrel of a lever-action Winchester rifle that was aimed directly at the viewer, who was, in this case, me. I stopped to study the photo for a moment and realized that the man in the photo was Woody.

I hadn't recognized him right away, because I'd never seen Woody wearing anything but the same type of tan work shirt and pants he always wore before he had retired some years earlier. And it was unusual to see him not in the company of his wife, Marva. They had buried Marva a month earlier, and there, in front of the photo studio, I thought of your remark that people were wondering what would become of Woody now that she was gone.

When Bob and I became old enough to ride our bicycles to the depot, you sometimes let us sit at the bay window work area where your Western Union telegraph equipment was located. Occasionally, when I sat at that desk and looked out the bay window toward the southwest, I would see Woody and Marva crossing the tracks on their walk to town. In fact, I never saw one without the other. Woody and Marva were inseparable, man and wife—or, in this case, wife and man.

Marva always led the way on their walks through town. She was a stout and bulky woman and walked with a slow, deliberate gait. Woody ambled along behind her with his eyes fixed on her back; he seemed to be waiting for her to signal where they were going or what they'd be doing next.

When Marva died, there was, as you said, a good deal of speculation about what Woody would do without her. I couldn't picture Woody walking on Main Street—or doing anything else—without Marva in the vanguard. Woody did drop out of sight for a few weeks, but when he made his debut as a widower, we saw a Woody Kettel that no one had ever met before.

I came upon Woody in person the day after I'd stared at his surprising portrait. He had forsaken the tan shirt and pants and now wore the fancy Hollywood cowboy suit I'd seen in the photo. He had added some accessories: a red bandanna around the neck and a gun belt supporting two holsters. In one, Woody carried a large Gene Autry cap pistol; in the other holster, he stored a spare bandanna. He wore tall, old-fashioned cowboy boots and had stuffed the pants of his costume in them, which drew the eye to his spindly bowlegs.

I knew that you were amused by Woody's choice of attire, but I don't think that you or anyone else had anticipated the bizarre turn his behavior would take. Bob and I probably knew about it before you and Isabel did, since you spent the evenings relaxing on the front porch. We had heard that he'd begun to entertain people downtown. He'd become the town jester, wandering up and down the two blocks of the business district performing highly amusing routines. One of the older boys told Bob and me that he had watched as Woody peered into the liquor store and pool hall and quacked like a duck at the patrons inside.

The first time I saw Woody in action was on a Friday night when Bob and I were downtown to see a double feature and a serial episode at the Republic Theater. Several people were standing near the ticket window, smiling, watching Woody. He had lately begun to station himself in front of the theater, hailing passing cars and watching moviegoers buy their tickets from Irene Martin inside the ticket booth. Gone was the meek little man Republic had known in the past. He'd become the charming host. As ticket-buyers completed their transactions, he would escort them to the entrance, where he would admit them by bowing deeply and sweeping his hat off in a grand gesture.

If there was a line at the ticket window, Woody entertained the waiting customers, improvising a stiff, jerky buck-and-wing dance number on the sidewalk. I loved to watch this rickety routine, which he sometimes embellished with hand clapping, arm waving, finger snapping, leg slapping, and boot stomping. One night he had it all going; when we laughed at him he stopped and quick-drew his cap pistol, pointed it at us and mouthed, "pow."

As eccentric as Woody had become, we couldn't believe our ears when we heard he had shot himself in the head down by the highway. But the eyewitness account of the event revealed it to be not tragic but bizarre and amusing. Woody had taken his "act" north to the intersection of Main Street and Highway 174, where the Trailways buses from Springfield turned to drive into Republic's downtown area.

According to the eyewitness, Woody had taken a position at the intersection from which he would be clearly visible to the bus driver and passengers on the left side of the bus. As the bus slowed and turned onto Main Street, Woody pulled the large Gene Autry cap pistol from its holster, pointed it at his temple, "fired" it, and fell, apparently lifeless, into the weeds beside the pavement.

Of course, Woody's "suicide" frightened the life out of the poor bus drivers and passengers the first time or two he staged it. The buses screeched to a stop, and people ran to his aid. They were not always amused when he suddenly jumped to his feet and did his little dance for them.

Woody became a celebrity around town—which encouraged him to continue his daily performances at the intersection. I liked your wry comment that Woody's death scenes had become the most interesting aspect of traveling to Republic by bus. But once they had caught on to Woody's act, the bus drivers began to warn their passengers as the bus approached the intersection. Even so, there were probably a few poor riders who nearly fainted when they saw an old man committing suicide outside their windows.

One afternoon, several of us walked to Main and Highway 174 to watch Woody shoot himself. We stood just out of sight so that he wouldn't be inhibited by the sight of the boys who usually teased him. He was pacing back and forth on the gravel shoulder of the highway and kicking at rocks while he waited for the bus. Suddenly, he looked up and scurried to another position. The Trailways bus was coming. Woody stood stiffly, waiting. I could hear the hissing of air brakes as the bus driver down-shifted the transmission to slow the bus. As the bus turned onto Main Street, Woody waved at the passengers to get their attention. Then he yanked the cap pistol from its holster, pointed it at his head, and fell onto the ground, where he lay very still.

This bus didn't stop, but the reaction of the passengers was still interesting. Some of the faces showed shock and horror; others paid no heed to Woody. They obviously were regular riders. While we were taking all of this in, Woody leaped to his feet, pointed at the passengers, and cackled in his thin, high voice. He performed his buck-and-wing for a few seconds, then abruptly turned and began to stroll casually down the sidewalk toward town.

I don't remember how long Woody's performances continued. It seems that he performed for months, during which time we tired of watching and teasing him: we had become distracted by more important matters involving girls.

Some people in the community might have thought Woody Kettel was an embarrassment to Republic. I didn't. In our town, eccentric behavior such as his wasn't universal, but it wasn't that unusual, either. When Woody's metamorphosis occurred, you mentioned that it saddened you to think that during all those years with Marva, there was something in Woody that needed to come out. Maybe what came out was surprising and slightly mad, but it didn't hurt anyone. Not even Woody, as he lay laughing in the weeds beside the highway.

Don

Bad Apples

Dear Jud:

It isn't that I dislike apples. I *can* eat them, and frequently do—varieties that you never knew: Fuji apples from New Zealand, Galas from Washington state, and Jonagolds that combine the best traits of the Jonathans and the Golden Delicious apples you favored. Today, food markets I patronize also still sell the varieties that grew around Republic—Rome, Red Delicious, Macintosh and Winesap.

Bob and I gorged on those juicy spheres every fall—which may be one reason my enthusiasm for them has waned. But as tasty as I find them now and then, there's something vaguely disturbing about apples. It must be that I associate them with apple orchards—the places in which Bob and I, looking for apples, often found trouble instead.

Let me recall an example: If it had not been for Winston Sears, his reputed memory lapses, and his apple orchard near the highway leading southwest to Billings, Bob and I probably would not have wrecked our 1934 Ford on the highway leading northeast to Springfield. I can now tell you how all that happened and include some details that we might have left out of our explanations in 1950.

During a morning trip to the post office, you had run into Winston, who had just got his hair cut at Shrimp Bennett's barber shop. Winston mentioned to you that he needed three apple pickers, and you remarked that you knew two sixteen-year-old boys who weren't busy. On your advice, Winston then called Isabel, who, of course, immediately promised that Bob and I would report to the orchard early the next morning. We were furious. We didn't want to ruin summer vacation days by working.

Since Winston still needed a third picker, we called Ron Gammon, who at first was not enthusiastic. But Bob and I had a plan; when Ron heard it and found no fault with it, he agreed to join us in the morning.

Shortly after you began your walk to the depot the next morning, Ron arrived at our house. The three of us climbed into our 1934 Ford and drove to Main Street. I glanced resentfully toward your depot as we turned left and proceeded to the highway that led to the apple orchard. Winston was expecting us. He outfitted each of us with a huge canvas bag and one of those ladders that are pointed at the top end to make it easier to thrust them up through the apple tree branches. They looked like gigantic, inverted crutches—which, although we didn't know it yet, was ominously prophetic.

"Go to it, boys! Get to pickin'!" Winston said, cheerily. We walked glumly into the grove of trees toward our picking area. I noticed that several women were already up in the tree branches busily plucking apples and thrusting them into their canvas bags. They stood easily on the rungs of their ladders, and I stared at their white legs beneath the hems of their light cotton dresses. Several other pickers on the ground were dragging canvas bags already bulging with apples at this early hour. I had picked apples previously only for my own pleasure, and this did not look like fun.

I thrust my ladder up into a tree, climbed the rungs, and began to pick. It was tedious work. It made my neck ache, and I found that I had to climb down frequently to manhandle the ladder into new picking positions. By 11 o'clock , I was full of despair. I had planned to spend this morning differently. My notion of the ideal morning was to sleep late and take a leisurely breakfast, after which I would retire to the living room couch in time to listen to Bob Poole on his *Poole's Paradise* radio broadcast from Chicago.

The three of us had discussed our plan the night before. We had heard that Winston was forgetful at times. He had once driven his truck to Springfield, it was said, and, after completing his business there, he rode the Trailways bus back to Republic—leaving his truck in Springfield. If the stories were true, we reasoned, he might not remember that he'd hired us and, therefore, wouldn't miss us if we left.

From my perch in the apple tree, I heard Bob's stealthy voice below. "Let's go, guys," he whispered. I quickly slid down the ladder and abandoned my apple bag, which was less than half full. During a trip to the water cooler, Ron had seen Winston drive away from the orchard in his pickup truck. So, it was now or never. We walked quickly toward the edge of the orchard, and, as we did, one of the younger women called to us from a nearby tree. "You boys finished so soon?" And from another tree, an older-sounding female voice said, "Um mmm! We like our men to have a little more staying power!" Both women laughed loudly as we walked through the dust to our waiting Ford.

I jumped behind the wheel and made a huge dust cloud as we sped away from the orchard. I took Highway 60 around the south side of Republic, hoping to minimize our chances of being seen by Winston or you. I drove through the *Y* and headed toward Springfield. Bob was in love with the waitress at the Highway 60 Café near Brookline and suggested that we celebrate our freedom there with hamburgers and french fries.

After a ten-minute drive, I turned into the café's gravel parking area and stopped near the backstop of the deteriorating softball diamond adjacent to the café. Once the home field of the mighty Brookline elementary school softball team, the diamond was seldom used now, and weeds were reaching up between the planks of the single stand of bleachers.

I stared through the chicken-wire backstop at the overgrown softball field and thought about the games our Republic grade school fast-pitch softball team had played here. As the team's catcher, I'd been on the receiving end of Gordon Stewart's fearsome curves and fastballs. For a time, with Gordon pitching, and the big bats of Wayne Garton and Charles Comisky, we had been unbeatable. Now, I gazed through the chicken-wire backstop and remembered the afternoon we lost to Brookline after they unveiled their secret weapons: Jimmy Chastain and Lester Davis. Both were pitchers, and both had blazing speed the equal of Gordon's. Since Gordon was our own pitcher and we seldom batted against him, we were unaccustomed to facing fastballers of that caliber. Their coach alternated Jimmy and Lester at the mound, while Gordon had to go it alone. He pitched heroically, but they simply outlasted him and beat us by a couple of runs.

That had been a sad day. But I was older now, and this day offered the promise of unknown adventure. I followed Bob and Ron into the café, where we found a booth by a window facing the highway. Ron and I ordered hamburgers and chocolate malts. Bob chose to eat at the counter, where he could watch the pretty, dark-haired waitress place her orders with the kitchen. While Ron and I ate, Bob sat on a stool at the counter and gazed soulfully at the girl as she moved about serving the few other diners in the cafe. I kept thinking that, later in the day, you or Isabel would ask us how much money we had made picking apples. We would either have to admit that we had left early or lie to you with some fictitious account of our day in the orchard.

Bob's girl finished her shift just before two o'clock. She had errands to do and had to leave, so the three of us decided to kill the rest of the afternoon at Ron's house in Republic.

Bob drove the Ford toward Republic, and, as we approached the truck-weighing station on the highway, he spotted a large billboard advertising women's swimsuits. The main illustration, of course, depicted a curvy blond in a tight-fitting suit that emphasized her best features. Bob called our attention to the billboard and all eyes, including his, were on the illustration until the instant before we crashed into the rear of a tractor-trailer rig. Absorbed in our admiration of the babe on the billboard, we had failed to notice the big rig lumbering away from the weighing station and onto the highway.

Ron spotted the truck first. When I heard him shout, "Look out!" I looked from the backseat through the windshield and saw a vast, gray wall rushing toward us. It was the rear of the trailer. When we hit it, the impact threw me over the seat, and my head struck the metal dashboard of our Ford. The weight and momentum of my body smashed Bob's seat forward, pinning him against the steering wheel. Ron, who was in the front passenger seat, was able to brace himself against the dashboard. By some miracle, he wasn't severely injured—except for some badly strained shoulders.

People do odd things in moments of crisis. I guess I had momentarily been knocked senseless by the blow to my forehead, because in the stillness that followed the crash, I opened the rear door on my side, got out, ran across the highway, sat down in a ditch, got up, and ran back to the car. Ron was tugging at Bob's door, and I began to help. My ears were ringing loudly and I still hadn't seen the massive lump on my forehead.

Bob was trapped in the car. The back of his seat seemed impossibly close to the steering wheel, which was curved slightly around his chest. Ron and I finally were able to rip the driver's seat away from the floor and help Bob out. I could smell a mixture of steaming antifreeze and oil and saw that the front of our beloved Ford was an unrecognizable tangle of metal. Dozens of metal fragments and components were scattered over the highway.

The rest of what I remember is a series of incongruities: a neatly uniformed Missouri state trooper using a push broom to sweep the remnants of our car to the edge of the highway; another patrolman writing my description of the wreck in a notebook, and, when I said the truck had darted in front of us, his comment that "it's kind of hard for trailer trucks to dart"; Bob, smiling and chatting with ambulance attendants as they rolled him toward their vehicle; my front-seat ride in the ambulance as we sped, siren whining, through a pleasant neighborhood in Springfield.

What surprised me most, I think, was the size of the lump on my head. It looked like someone had sawed a hard-boiled egg in half and glued one of the halves above my right eyebrow. When

Bob saw me, he wanted to laugh, but his bruised ribs made that too painful.

A number of Republic residents had come upon the steaming wreckage of our Ford, had seen the ambulance, and had recognized us. Apparently one or more of these witnesses was overwrought and took back fantastic—and faulty—reports that Bob, Ron, and I had been killed on the highway. More accurate reports quickly followed, but I'm still sorry that you and Isabel had had to suffer the shock of hearing that initial report.

I'm glad that Ron's dad called to tell you that our injuries hadn't been serious and that he would drive to the hospital in Springfield and bring us home. When we returned like Lazaruses late that afternoon, you and Isabel were waiting on the front porch—and you were gladder to see us than I had expected you would be earlier in the day.

We were celebrities for the evening, but that faded away the next morning when the insurance adjuster came. Our account of the accident wasn't convincing to him, either. He stopped writing and said, "I'm having a little trouble with that 'darting trailer truck' description, boys." I knew as soon as the interview was over that we wouldn't be receiving an insurance check with which to replace our Ford. That made me feel bad enough. What made me feel worse was that I knew our answers were untruthful and that the insurance man knew it, too.

You said that Bob and I would have to go without a car for the time being, and we did— for months and months. In time, I began to see that the whole experience—avoiding our obligations, wrecking our car, dabbling in obfuscation—was a lesson about responsibility. And if you had later graded me on how much I had learned from that lesson, you probably would have given me at least a B.

I associate apples with some other unpleasant incidents, including an exceptionally hard punch in the mouth and a shotgun blast to the rear of our car.

I felt that I had given you a good answer the morning you asked why my lip was purple and larger than usual. My reply was vague but not totally untruthful. I told you that, during the previous night, some boys had been throwing apples, and one of them hit me. I wanted you to interpret that as meaning one of the apples had hit me. You said, "Um hm." And I saw that you clearly understood what had really happened.

It had been one of those small-town summertime nights. Ron Gammon and I were driving around town in the 1936 Studebaker sedan that Bob and I had purchased to replace our shattered Ford. Another vehicle began to follow us. I heard a thump on the roof of my car and saw an apple falling to the pavement ahead of us. Then there was another thump, and another. The vehicle behind us, a pickup truck, was full of boys and they were bombing us with apples.

I drove into the parking area of the truck stop and café at the end of West Elm and rolled down my window. When the pickup pulled up beside us, I told the occupants they were "bastards and jackasses." There were five of them and only two of us, so I was at first relieved when I saw only one of the apple-throwers climb out of the pickup.

But then I heard Ron mutter, "Oh, shit!" The boy who was walking rapidly toward us was an amateur boxer who had won a number of club titles—several of them by knockouts. He leaned toward my window and asked if I wanted to retract my comments since he took special offense to the word, "jackass." I said something to the effect that there wouldn't be any retraction and that my comment stood. He yanked the door open and dragged me out by my shirtsleeve. We stood facing each other, and he said something along the lines of, "Okay, now what was it you called me?" I looked at him and said that I believed him to be a stupid jackass.

That was the moment I discovered that being knocked out wasn't nearly as painful as I had always imagined it would be. The only sensation I can recall is that of skidding on my back through gravel. I saw nothing but blackness for a moment or two, then the blackness became the night sky with stars above. I heard steps crunching toward me and the boxer's voice saying that if I didn't get up he would kick my head off. I was alert enough to decide that getting up and being knocked down again wouldn't hurt nearly as much as staying down and having my head kicked off. So I got up.

I was swaying on my feet but I managed to stay upright. The boxer again asked me to take back my remark. Under the circumstances, I was surprised at the anger I felt, and I told him to go to hell. I then watched him carefully, because I hadn't seen either of his arms move before his last punch. But he simply looked at me for a moment, shook his head and walked away.

My knees were shaking so violently I could barely walk back to my car. As we were driving away, I said that I felt pretty good about facing down the boxer. Ron explained how that had happened. He said that he had heard the boxer tell the others that he wanted to knock me down again but that I looked so bad he was ashamed of himself.

Later that summer, Bob and I decided to give the Studebaker a workout on a nighttime watermelon raid. When darkness fell, we crowded several friends into the "Stude" and drove to the watermelon field north of the high school. This patch was adjacent to the apple orchard which was nestled in the *Y*—the fork where Highway 174 joined Highway 60. Bob drove and demonstrated the old car's surprisingly good performance. Our friends expressed admiration and approval. During the short trip, we discussed our strategy. We would park the Stude on the gravel road in front of the watermelon patch—ready for a quick getaway in case that became necessary. We would employ stealth because we had heard rumors that the owner sometimes guarded the field at night. Therefore, we would enter the adjacent apple orchard in a flanking maneuver and, from there, creep into the melon field unseen, we hoped.

The dark cover of the apple orchard gave way to an open sky, and the rows of melons stood out clearly in the bright moonlight. I felt a little uneasy, but we crept forward into the field and soon each of us had a large melon under one arm. That is when it happened.

Bright light from several floodlights suddenly illuminated the field. I heard a man's voice shouting, then a shotgun blast followed by the sound of rock-salt pellets whooshing overhead. We dropped the melons we had plucked, jumped to our feet, and sprinted across the patch toward the road and the safety of our car. I heard another, different, voice and then another roar from the shotgun. The pellets seemed to pass closer overhead this time, and I realized that the watermelon guards were chasing us. We vaulted the wire fence and had just clambered into the Studebaker when one of the guards fired one more blast at us. The pellets struck the back of the car full force, removing most of the black enamel from the trunk, a flaw you noticed the next day.

I gunned the engine and the Studebaker lurched forward, leaving a shower of gravel and a thick cloud of dust that probably concealed our departure and may have averted yet another shotgun blast. We flew over the gravel road until we reached Highway 60, where I turned left and headed toward Springfield. In the back seat, Wayne Garton was doing a head count, and noticed that Buzz Mueller was missing. So, I wheeled the old car around and drove back toward the apple orchard.

The eastern edge of the orchard paralleled the highway, and as we drew near, I turned off the headlights. Then I remembered that we were still on the highway and pulled onto the shoulder, where I let the Studebaker roll to a stop. Our only illumination came from the moon, and we strained our eyes hoping we'd see some sign of Buzz.

Suddenly, there was movement in one of the trees at the edge of the orchard. A figure dropped to the ground and ran toward us. It was Buzz. He nearly pulled the rear door off its hinges in his haste to open it, and he dived onto the bodies huddled in the back seat.

I ground the transmission into low gear and swerved back onto the highway, heading south toward Billings. As we raced away, Buzz explained how he had become separated from us in the panic that followed the first volley from the shotgun. He said that while we ran, he flattened himself between two rows of watermelon vines and heard two men run by in pursuit. While they were busy trying to take the paint off the rear of the Studebaker, he slithered from the field and into the orchard. He first ran through the trees toward the highway, then decided to climb into one of the trees to wait until things calmed down a bit.

During the brief time we had been driving toward Springfield thinking that Buzz was with us, he had been crouching high in the branches of the apple tree. He said that he was just beginning to believe he would survive the night when he heard footsteps below. The two guards had dashed to the edge of the orchard, hoping to get off one more shot if we drove by on the highway. The two men were laughing, and Buzz heard one say, "We scared the crap outa them little piss ants, didn't we?" At that point, Buzz said, his heart was beating so fast he hyperventilated and almost fell from the tree right on top of them.

He managed to cling to his perch, and the men, fortunately, never thought to look upward. They walked away just moments before Buzz spotted the Studebaker creeping slowly through the moonlight to his rescue.

I really should admit that not all of my apple-related experiences were unpleasant. In 1938, before there was a highway to intersect it, Elm Street became a country road just beyond the Haynes House, where we lived, and for miles, the road followed the hilly landscape that rolled eastward toward Springfield. On a balmy, golden fall afternoon, Isabel trusted her four-year-old twins to play without supervision in the front yard. It was one of those mistakes that parents sometimes make.

We played contentedly for a short time. Then, since Isabel wasn't there to stop us, we left the yard and began to walk eastward on Elm Street and on along the dirt road. We followed the country road for a short time and soon reached the edge of an apple orchard, which was on the north side of the road behind a wire fence. I climbed the fence to look into the orchard. There were rows and rows of trees, and it seemed to be a place that offered adventure. We crawled over the fence and wandered into the orchard. It was wonderful. The sunlight was mellow, and the cool air was sweet with the fragrance of apples. The two of us proceeded into the shady orchard, and soon we were squandering apples. We'd select a luscious-looking apple, take a bite or two, then toss it aside when we spotted another, choicer specimen on the ground.

Since we were paying no attention at all to our surroundings, we soon were lost. I began to feel a prickle of fear when I discovered that whichever way I turned, nothing looked familiar. So we continued on through the orchard until the row through which we were walking ended at another wire fence that separated the orchard from a broad field. Across that field sat a farmhouse.

I could see the back porch of the house and, as I looked, a screen door banged open and a woman came out onto the porch to hang a wash tub on the wall of the house. When she turned, she saw us watching her, and she motioned for us to come over. So we climbed the fence and walked to the porch.

We didn't know the woman, but since we were dressed as twins, she knew to whom we belonged. She held the screen door open and invited us into her kitchen.

Even before stepping onto the porch, I had smelled an apple pie baking. Inside the woman's kitchen, the pie's aroma filled my nose. The woman smiled at us and told us to take a seat at the kitchen table while she used her telephone. I watched her crank her wall telephone, and I wondered how she knew to tell the operator to connect her to the Aldermans' house. In a moment, the woman said "Hello, Mrs. Alderman," and then she explained who she was, how we had shown up at her house, and how Isabel could get there.

When the woman hung up the telephone, she told us that our mom would be coming soon and that we should have a piece of fresh apple pie while we waited. She put plates in front of us and then placed huge wedges of steaming apple pie on them. She plopped slivers of yellow cheese on each piece and asked if we liked cheese on our pie. I had never tried it, but I told her I liked it. And when I tasted the cheese and pie together, I discovered that I did like it.

I happily ate my pie and looked around the woman's kitchen. Her sink had no faucets. Instead, there was a small water pump next to the sink, and when she moved the handle up and down, water poured from the spout. A breeze blew in through the window above the sink, and I could smell the red bar of Lifebuoy soap that I saw on the windowsill. The breeze came again and blew the window curtains open, and through the window, I saw the Old Dodge coming up the dirt lane toward the farmhouse.

The woman stepped out onto the back porch, and I heard her voice first and then Isabel's voice. The two of them came into the kitchen, and when Isabel saw us, she shook her head and apologized to the woman for her trouble. The woman said we were no trouble at all, and she served us another piece of pie while they visited. In a little while, we were riding in the Old Dodge again, heading home.

Well, Jud, this will be a good point to end this letter, because the memory of that afternoon is the best thing I can tell you about apples and orchards.

Don

Dear Jud:

I have a theory about F. H. Denver's retirement as city marshal. I believe that if he had stayed on a few more years, at least a couple of episodes that are part of Republic's lore might never have occurred.

For example, with F.H. patrolling the downtown blocks, someone wouldn't have felt free to leave a car containing a dead body parked just off Main Street, across from your depot. And poor, mad Elton Jennings wouldn't have been allowed to terrorize the town, waving a pistol with which he had planned to shoot the man whom he claimed had swindled him out of a fortune.

When you brought home the news that F.H. was retiring, you said you wondered if Republic even needed another marshal since most people in town were such peaceable folks. But I do think that his reputation had something to do with the fact that the years of his service were so peaceful. What lawbreaker would want to risk a confrontation with a city marshal strong enough to lift a full-grown horse nearly a foot off the ground and good enough with a pistol to shoot a hole through a playing card that he'd tossed into the air?

The fact is, as our town marshal, F.H. never needed to use those abilities. The knowledge that he had them was probably enough to deter lawbreakers to the extent that he served Republic basically as a night watchman who peered into store windows at night and checked doors to make sure merchants hadn't forgotten to lock them. The boredom of this routine was relieved only occasionally by some minor disturbance of the peace. And even these disturbances were, in a way, routine. They usually occurred at Juggy's Place, where overstimulated pool hall regulars had taken to swinging their pool cues at each other. Billy Burris's heckling of the pool players usually precipitated one of these brawls, which quickly ended when F.H. arrived to escort Billy to Republic's wretched jail, conveniently located just steps away in the alley behind Juggy's.

You and Isabel kept an eye out for another troublemaker who, although he meant no harm, was a potential hazard to us when we played our nighttime street games. From the front porch in the soft light of early evening you had a wide-angle view of Elm Street. And when you saw Joe Ed Dean cruising toward town on his gray Ford tractor, you yelled at us to move our games to the backyard or some other location away from Joe Ed's return route. You remembered that after a previous evening of beer-drinking at Juggy's, Joe Ed had climbed onto his tractor for the drive back to the farm east of Republic where he worked. On that return trip, Joe Ed hadn't actually driven *on* Elm Street. Just past the deep ditch adjacent to the lumber yard, Joe Ed had veered off the pavement to drive his tractor on the sidewalk and on through people's front lawns—ours included.

After your warning that night, I had stood on the porch to watch Joe Ed's approach to our property. The tractor's distant headlights traced an erratic path as he drove on the sidewalk in front of Grace Land's house, swerved left onto Fred Owen's property, continued on through Doc O'Dell's yard, then through Edna Egan's, and Tishy O'Dell's, Ed Huckins's, and Ab Norman's. At this point, the lights swerved back onto the sidewalk and I knew he was passing in front of the haunted house. Once past that obstacle, Joe Ed turned back into the field adjacent to our house, and, as he tore across our lawn and on through the Cantrells' yard, he was singing "I'm Walking the Floor Over You."

F.H. inherited the city marshal/night watchman job from old Jim Perkins. I remember Jim most for killing our dog in the middle of Main Street—a kinder act than it sounds. Jim was a big man, and he had quelled a few fights at Juggy's. But he was in his mid-to-late seventies and was undoubtedly content to walk through the downtown area, rattling locked doors and peering into store windows, until it was time to return to his storefront living quarters next to Eagan's Market.

On the day Jim Perkins had to kill T.C., our dog, we had walked to the depot to visit you, since you were fond of the mutt and amused by his name. You said you'd never known a dog called by initial letters. After you and Isabel said we could keep the stray that had appeared in our front yard, we set about trying to name him. His fur was a mottled black, white, and brown, which inspired Bob to suggest "Three Colors" as a suitable and logical name. I agreed, and we soon shortened the name to "T.C.," which was easier to yell when we were calling him home.

Lucille Mitchell happened by one morning while Bob and I were on the front sidewalk grooming T.C. She stopped to look at our pooch, and the dialog between her and Bob went something like this:

"I see you boys have a new dog, What's his name?"

"T.C."

"T.C.? What does T.C. stand for?"

"Three colors."

"Oh, good Lord!" And she continued on down the street.

But as I had begun to say, the three of us were walking on the sidewalk on the west side of Main Street when T.C. suddenly decided there was urgent dog business on the east side. Dashing across the street, he failed to notice a fast-moving dump truck. The wheels of the heavy truck ran over poor T.C., crushing his hindquarters, and he lay in agony on the pavement, biting at the sky. Jim witnessed the accident, and, moving nimbly for a man his age, dashed over to comfort us and tell us that he needed to "put the poor critter out of his misery." His eyes were kind and regretful when he looked at us. He then borrowed a heavy ball-peen hammer from the dump-truck driver and dispatched T.C. with two blows to the head. I ran to my favorite meditating tree near Harold Owen's house and spent the rest of the day high in the comforting embrace of its branches.

When Jim Perkins retired in 1944, you reported one evening that the city council had chosen F. H. Denver to take over as city marshal. There probably wasn't much discussion about other candidates, if there were any. F.H. seemed the logical choice. He was a marksman with his pistol and he was powerfully muscled after years of heavy work as Republic's blacksmith.

For years, F.H. had shod horses for the farmers and repaired their wagons, cultivators, and hay rakes. He also sharpened lawnmowers, which is how Bob and I came to meet him in 1942. You let us walk with you when you rolled our steel-wheeled mower downtown to see if F.H. could sharpen its rusty old blades.

F. H. Denver's eroded brick building had housed a livery and wagon business in the early nineteen hundreds. It later became a blacksmith shop, and F.H. purchased the business in the thirties, just before you and Isabel moved to Republic. His smithing customers brought their horses and farm equipment to an oil-soaked, hard-packed receiving yard on the south side of the building. But you rolled our mower through the door fronting Main Street. When I first peered into the shop, I saw a jumble of shadowy metal shapes: Some were machines waiting to be fixed. Other shapes were machines that did the fixing. The interior was dimly illuminated by several bare incandescent bulbs at the ends of cords that disappeared into darkness overhead. The only other illumination was provided by daylight that came in through the big receiving door.

F.H. was busy pounding a glowing red horseshoe on the anvil. He squinted his eyes against the heat, and his mouth was turned down in an expression of total concentration. But when he turned to see who his customers were, his mouth straightened wide across his face, and grin-wrinkles appeared at the sides of his eyes. He held up a finger to signal he'd be with us in a minute and resumed working to shape the horseshoe to a certain horse's hoof. He used huge, long tongs to thrust the U-shaped piece of metal into the brick forge, cranking the bellows until the air and heat turned the horseshoe shimmering red. He then placed the shoe on the anvil again and pieces of hot metal flaked off as he pounded away in his peculiar, clanging rhythm.

When the shoe was shaped to suit him, F.H. plunged it into a tank of black-looking water to cool it, and a cloud of acrid steam rose up. The steamy atmosphere of the shop was a conglomeration of odors: the smells of horses, filings from their hooves, F.H.'s sweat, and coal smoke from the forge. F.H. grabbed an odd-looking hammer, walked to a waiting horse, and pulled the animal's front leg up and clamped it between his own legs. Holding the horse's leg tightly, he placed the new horseshoe on the hoof and secured it with nails that he fished from an apron pocket. He held the horse's hoof so that we could see the new shoe in place. "See?" he said. "Perfect fit, by God! Now, what can I do fer you gents?"

Later that year, Bob and I were at the tire repair business, across the packed dirt lot from the blacksmith shop, visiting with Ikey Holder and some other older boys. F.H. emerged from his building and walked toward us, holding a pistol. One of the boys asked F.H. if he was going to shoot us. F.H. grinned and said he wouldn't waste bullets on us but he would show us a trick. He told us to stand back, and he looked in all directions to make sure that everything was clear. With his left hand, he pulled a playing card from the pocket of his overalls and flipped it high into the air. His right arm snapped up and he aimed the pistol at the airborne card. There was a loud report, and the card leaped toward the sky before fluttering to the ground. Ikey picked the card up and whistled. When he held it up for us, we saw that it was an ace of spades with a neat hole through it.

On another occasion, Bob and I were in F.H.'s shop, watching him shoe a horse. One by one, he began to attach the custom-shaped horseshoes with square nails that he pounded into each hoof. The horse became skittish when F.H. bent to clamp one of the rear hooves between his legs. He patted the horse on its flank and spoke soothingly, which seemed to calm the animal. As he resumed his shoeing, F.H. grinned at us. "It's these rear legs you gotta watch," he said. "He could kick my ass clear to Christian County if I got careless."

He then squatted under the horse, placed his back against its belly and straightened until he had lifted the horse nearly a foot off the ground. The horse's eyes rolled wildly. After a moment, F.H. lowered the huge animal and let its hooves touch the ground again. He ducked out from under the horse and grinned at us, but the effort must have upset his stomach, because he suddenly stepped outside the shop and vomited onto the packed dirt.

By the time the city council approached F.H. about taking over Jim Perkins's job, F.H.'s blacksmithing business was in decline. Tractors and more advanced farm equipment were replacing the horses and their horse-drawn machines and wagons. So, from F. H.'s perspective, the time was right for a new career. He also admitted that he was getting too old for the heavy labor of blacksmithing. So, we soon became accustomed to seeing F.H. visiting with the merchants in the afternoon and peering into their store windows at night.

Elevators have made me nervous for as long as I can remember. Even now, when I step aboard one, I try not to think about the dark, deep shaft that lies beneath my feet. Part of my apprehension about elevators, or more specifically, elevator shafts, stems from Isabel's dire warnings of what could happen to us if we stood too close to the elevator doors in Heer's department store. But I can also trace my misgivings to an incident in which F.H. may have saved my life.

I never mentioned that elevator incident to you or Isabel because I thought it would confirm your suspicions that I wasn't very bright. It occurred on a summer night when F.H. allowed Bob and me to accompany him on his rounds. We walked with him as he checked all the stores on Main Street. Then the three of us walked through the lumber yard property, checking doors at the building there; then we proceeded across the street to the old cold-storage building. It was during World War II and your Frisco freight trains brought in vast amounts of commodities to be stored in the massive four-story building. It was F.H.'s job to check the four floors of the storage facility every night.

I was excited but a little apprehensive because I'd never been inside this huge, windowless pile of bricks. He unlocked a heavy door, and we stepped into a large, dusty-smelling room. In the dim, yellowish light, I could see burlap bags of grain or beans or other goods stacked tall in rows that extended into the gloom. F.H. told us to wait while he checked out this storeroom. He disappeared down one row, and I could see only the beam of his flashlight as he aimed it up and down the stacks of materials. In a short time he emerged from another row, and said, "Okay, let's go check the next floor."

He led us to the building's big open-fronted freight elevator, and, after we stepped onto the platform, he operated the controls. I heard the whining of an electric motor high above us, and the platform began to rise slowly up the dark, musty shaft. When we reached the second floor, F.H. repeated the inspection process, and we were back aboard the elevator. This is when it happened. As we rose toward the third floor, I stuck my head out the open front to look down into the yawning, black pit beneath us. I was frozen by the sight of the black hole under us, and wasn't aware that my head was about to strike the edge of the oncoming floor. Suddenly, I heard F.H.'s voice, and felt myself being yanked away from the front of the elevator. "Don't ever do that!" he yelled. "That could of sheared your head off! Or worse yet, knocked you into the shaft—and there's no tellin' what you'd land on when you hit bottom!" I stood at the back of the elevator during the rest of our tour. And to this day, when I ride an elevator, I can't let my thoughts dwell on the dark and empty space beneath me.

F.H. became as familiar a figure downtown as Mr. Peavey and Woody Kettel, and he was still marshal when we entered high school. We saw him sometimes making his rounds on foot, but, more and more often, he began to patrol the streets in the second-hand Hudson he had purchased at about the time you bought the second-hand Nash. If we were downtown at night, walking home from the Republic Theater or just roaming, we could expect to see F.H. sitting alone in his Hudson on Main Street. He kept a large thermos of coffee, from which he drank while he listened to the radio. Usually, he waved a greeting to us from his car, but sometimes he seemed not to see us. I wondered how he could tolerate such a lonely job.

One Halloween night, I learned what it was like to be afraid of the law. Bob, Gary Baumberger, Ron Gammon, and I had decided it would be hilarious to switch the business signs identifying Republic's two doctor's offices. We removed the sign that read "Carl Leidinger, MD" and placed it in front of the office of Doc Mitchell, the osteopath. We then replaced Dr. Leidinger's sign with one reading "R. C. Mitchell, OD." We hoped it would displease them both.

Apparently F.H. spotted us just as we finished securing Dr. Mitchell's sign to Dr. Leidinger's Main Street office. We heard the sound of a car engine starting and looked up to see the Hudson driving toward us. We dashed away north on Main Street, ducking behind trees and bushes until we reached Anderson Avenue, where we turned and ran toward the high school. Behind me, I heard someone say, "Oh, shit!" F.H. had turned on Anderson and was following us. We hid behind more bushes and waited until his car passed by, then we ran to Pine Street and headed south again toward the business district. We thought we had lost him, but car lights appeared behind us and I realized that F.H. was seriously in pursuit. Pine Street ended at the railroad tracks, so we sprinted up the slope of the railroad bed and ran to our left along the tracks.

We knew that F.H. couldn't drive his Hudson on the rails, so we slowed to a walk, panting and laughing. We walked until we reached the athletic field behind the high school and left the tracks at that point to walk across the field toward the school buildings. But we hadn't walked far when we again saw headlights. F.H. had guessed our destination and was driving across the field in our direction. His headlights hadn't illuminated us, but we instinctively ran back toward the railroad and leaped over the embankment at the edge of the athletic field.

My heart was pounding as I flattened myself against the incline, my head just a few inches below the edge of the field. Above the thumping in my ears, I heard the sound of footsteps approaching, and I knew F.H. was very close. The powerful beam from his five-cell flashlight swept back and forth above our heads. He stood there forever, it seemed, aiming the bright shaft and just missing the tops of our heads. Finally, his footsteps moved away from us. We peeked over the edge of the embankment when we heard the sound of his car starting, and we watched him drive from the field and onto Anderson Avenue.

At that point, we decided that Halloween should be over. We separated and walked to our homes, still keeping an eye out for F.H. He apparently had tired of the chase, and we presumed that he had returned to his familiar parking spot on Main. But no one wanted to confirm that.

F. H. retired as city marshal the following year. That was the year that I took the summer job at LaVega Claiborn's Western Auto store downtown, which led to my coming literally within inches of finding the decomposed body of a man in that abandoned car.

My responsibilities as a Western Auto clerk included changing engine oil and fixing flats for customers, so I usually reported to work at the rear entrance of the store. On two mornings, as I walked across West Elm to enter the alley behind the buildings on the west side of Main, I had noticed an unfamiliar car. It was parked off of the pavement, nosed up against the wall of the building that had housed Roll Ottendorf's grocery store. My route took me near the car, and, as I walked past it on the third morning, I smelled something dead. I glanced around, looking for the carcass of a dog or cat nearby. I saw nothing, so I moved closer to the car and bent down to see if the dead animal was lying beneath the chassis. Again, I saw nothing, so I assumed that whatever was dead must be lying in the weeds adjacent to the building, and I continued on down the alley.

I was surprised to see you, Jud, when you came into the store just after LaVega had opened for business. Your face was pale, and you told us you'd just seen something you hoped you'd never see again. You said that Pearl Dial, a teenager I knew, had noticed a bad smell as she passed the car on her way to town. Unlike me, she was curious enough to look into the vehicle, and had discovered a dead man slumped on the backseat. She ran to the depot and burst into your office screaming about "a dead man across the street!"

When you followed her to the car, you saw the blackened, decomposing body inside. You said you'd gone back to the depot and called the Greene County sheriff's office in Springfield and that officers were on the way.

Later that morning, I was standing at the front of the store when I saw the mystery vehicle passing before my eyes. Four men, all wearing bandannas over their noses and mouths, were pushing the car slowly through town toward the new funeral home. One man steered the car through the open front window. The rear door on my side was open, and from it extended a leg, which bounced stiffly as the car rolled over the pavement.

That night, you described how sheriff's department investigators came to the depot and took down your account of finding the body. A story about the gruesome discovery in Republic appeared in one of the Springfield newspapers the next day. The article said it was likely that someone had shot the unidentified man and left him in the car, hoping that it would appear that he had shot himself. The authorities, however, were leaning toward homicide rather than suicide, since the weapon the man would have used was missing.

That incident caused a commotion in town for a week or so, and then everyone settled back into the somnolent rhythm of hot summer days.

But before the summer was over, we were jarred again when Elton Jennings, an out-of-town man, came to Republic to shoot a man no one had ever heard of. I'll never forget that day. I was working at the Western Auto store the morning Elton appeared on our streets looking for a man named Streetman. A couple of men who were stopped by Elton quickly passed the word that Elton believed this man lived in Republic and that he intended to shoot the man on sight for cheating him in a sizable financial transaction.

You later told us that you didn't realize anything out of the ordinary was happening until I called you from the Western Auto store. I had sprinkled sawdust soaked in engine oil over the store's concrete floor and had just begun my morning sweeping when Babe Dean rushed in. Babe breathlessly told LaVega Claiborn and me that Elton had "flipped his lid" and was walking around town with his gun drawn. Babe related the revenge story and stood in front of us, wide-eyed, glancing apprehensively toward the street.

I walked to the big plate glass window and looked out. Main Street seemed deserted. Then, another customer came in and said that the mayor had called the Greene County sheriff's headquarters in Springfield—since we didn't have a marshal at the moment— and that deputies were on their way to Republic.

The men were speculating about how the law officers might apprehend Elton and what kind of gun battle might ensue. I glanced out the plate-glass window again and spotted the shadow of an arm on the sidewalk. I jumped away from the window just as Elton himself came into view. He was, indeed, holding a pistol. I hid behind a hardware display case and watched him move closer to the store window. He shielded his eyes with one hand as he pressed his face against the glass and stared into the store. His eyes were squinted, and his mouth was drawn wide, showing two rows of teeth. He wasn't smiling.

Elton finally moved away from the window, and I feared that he was about to come into the store. I wondered if I would be able to dash behind counters and make it through the rear door of the store. But Elton must have satisfied himself that his enemy wasn't in the store, and he had walked away to search elsewhere. I looked behind me to say something to the men, but they were nowhere in sight.

Elton wandered on down Main Street, and, after a time, Babe Dean rushed into the store again to report that Elton had gone to a cousin's house at the edge of the business district and had locked himself inside, taking his cousin hostage. At about that time, a man I didn't know came in to say that patrol cars from the sheriff's department and the Missouri State Highway Patrol had taken positions near the house. The law officers had been told that Elton was armed, and they crouched behind their vehicles, calling for Elton to give up and come outside.

I walked just outside the entrance to the store and stood on the sidewalk, waiting to hear the sounds of a furious shoot-out. The men who were on their way to get as close as they dared to the hostage house wore strained expressions. I didn't feel afraid, but my face and arms were clammy. Main Street was very quiet. I heard only an occasional hoarse whisper as someone hurried by or the noise of a car rushing down a back street.

After you had talked to Isabel by telephone, you walked back to Western Auto for an update. We told you we had heard that the law officers were going to have to storm the house if Elton didn't come out soon and that things didn't look good. We agreed that if F.H. were still marshal, he probably would have ended things quickly. You chatted a few more minutes with LaVega, and then, telling me not to go close to the surrounded house, you returned to the depot.

Just after you left, Buddy Cook, who had been observing the standoff, ran into the store to say that it was all over. Doc Mitchell had walked to the front door of the house and asked Elton if he could come inside. Elton agreed, and while Doc was inside, he persuaded Elton to take something that would calm his nerves. It was a powerful sedative that soon rendered him unconscious.

Doc then walked outside to tell the officers that everything was all right. Several officers entered the house, carried Elton outside, and placed him in an ambulance from Springfield, which smoothly sped away.

That day was the main topic of conversation in town for weeks—even months later, some people were still retelling it. There were different versions of the day's events, of course, but nearly every telling included a common theme: if F.H. Denver had still been on the job, the day's events probably wouldn't have happened. It was probably true. But in one sense that would have been a shame, because it would have made Republic a slightly less interesting place to live.

Don

Dear Jud:

You were right about Brenda. When I asked for the $75 I needed to make a down payment on an engagement ring, you said no. You said she wasn't the right girl for me and you weren't going to contribute to such folly.

I was angry and unable to understand that you had recognized something about her that I was too green to detect. I was twenty and about to report for active duty in the Navy Reserve. I wouldn't be seeing her for months, and I thought that if I gave her a ring, she would wait for me. Somehow, I came up with part of the $75, and she lent me the rest. I bought the ring and we became engaged.

That was in June 1954. In early December, a letter came to me at my barracks at Sand Point Naval Air Station in Seattle. It was a notice from the jewelry company, advising me that my fiancée had had the diamond I purchased reset on a more expensive band and that my payments would be going up.

Brenda had been writing to me less and less frequently, and her letters had been getting shorter and shorter. I sat on my bunk and thought about the letter from the jewelry company. Then I thought about her latest perfunctory note and the revelation came: I needed to get back to Missouri as soon as possible, obtain the ring from Brenda and pay her the money she'd invested, return the ring to the jewelers, and then forget about her.

A few days later, I learned that on December 22, a Navy P2V patrol bomber would be flying from our base to the Naval Air Station in Hutcheson, Kansas, which was about as close to Republic as the Navy could get me. I was able to arrange a few days of Christmas leave and reserve a place on the flight. By the time we arrived in Hutcheson, it was late at night. I was half-frozen because I'd had to ride in the aircraft's bomb bay, which was unheated, obviously. During the flight, I kept wondering if I might be lying over the bomb bay doors. I worried that someone in the aircraft's cockpit might accidentally nudge the button that opened the doors and that I would fall into the freezing blackness below, never to be heard of again.

But late that night we landed at the Hutcheson Naval Air Station without incident, and the crew members wished me luck as I climbed out of the bomber. They assured me that I'd have no problem hitchhiking to Kansas City on the highway that ran past the air station. A fierce winter wind whipped across the plains of Kansas as I walked along the dark highway, extending my thumb to the few vehicles that were still traveling on what was now December 23—the day before Christmas Eve. I finally caught a ride with a kindly driver who took me to the train station in Kansas City. Later that day, I took a train to Springfield and then a bus to Republic. You and Isabel were glad to see me when I walked up the front steps, happy that I'd be there for the Christmas holiday.

On the following day, I called Brenda to say I needed to talk to her. She didn't seem thrilled to hear from me, but she agreed to see me. I borrowed your 1947 Nash, since my 1951 Plymouth was in Seattle, and drove to Brenda's duplex apartment in Springfield. She didn't appear to be either surprised or disappointed when I told her I was there to reclaim the ring—which, I noticed, she was not wearing. She stared at me for a moment and said if I wanted the ring, I would have to come inside to get it.

As soon as I stepped through the door, I saw why she wanted me to come in. She had used holiday glitter paint to spray her new boyfriend's name on a large mirror in her living room. His name was framed by fanciful curlicues and embellishments which, apparently, she thought were appropriate to the season.

She returned from her bedroom with the ring in a jewelry box, and, when I offered to repay her share of the down payment, she refused, saying that, considering everything, it wouldn't be fair for me to have to do that. I thanked her and she accompanied me to the front door. We said goodbye and I sprang athletically down the steps and walked briskly to the car. I knew she was standing in the door watching me, but I didn't look back as I sped away.

From there, I drove directly to the jewelry company in downtown Springfield, where I explained my situation to the manager on duty, a pleasant-faced, balding man. He examined the engagement ring while he listened to my tale, and then he said, "I'm sorry to hear about your bad luck. We'll just call it even—okay?" I thanked him and left, feeling embarrassed but relieved.

With that unpleasantness out of the way, I was ready to celebrate my freedom, and the Christmas holidays. That night, I told you and Isabel that I had returned the ring to the jeweler's and that Brenda was no longer my fiancée. You told me that I had done the right thing. Isabel said the world was full of nice, pretty girls, and that I would meet one soon.

I slept well that night, and, when I awoke, I realized that it was Christmas Eve day. Since I had been away for months, you and Isabel, I know, were assuming that I'd spend Christmas Eve at home. But in my mind, I was a different person from the greenhorn I had been. I was now a Navy man, a traveler of some sophistication who had watched Lily St. Cyr dance in San Francisco. Although it was Christmas Eve, I needed to be out with other men of the world rather than with you and Isabel. I felt that a night out in Springfield might lead me to that girl I needed to meet.

So I called Ferd Robinson and Josh Mansfield and arranged to meet them at Stewart's Drive-In that evening. You (sadly, I thought) said I could have the Nash again, and, when it was time to leave the two of you, I felt a sharp pang of remorse. You had turned on the Christmas tree, the radio was playing carols, and under the tree I saw several packages with my name on the tags.

I drove to Springfield and met Ferd and Josh at the drive-in. Ferd had invited a friend named Paul Wilson to join us. Paul seemed good-natured and compatible. He also possessed another asset: a large bottle of peach brandy, which he said would keep us warm on this chilly Christmas Eve.

We had no plans, apart from the fantasy that somehow we would meet four gorgeous females at some point during the evening. We believed that the wholesome and attractive small-town girls we'd discover—the ones who were sure to be walking around downtown Springfield on Christmas Eve—would be easy prey if we posed as four lonely sailors just back from duty off the coast of North Korea with orders to report to Chicago for a special, high-security assignment. The more cryptic it sounded, the more intriguing it would be, we decided.

My three friends got into the Nash, and we began the drive that would lead us to our destiny. Looking back, I am reminded of our aimless odyssey each time I watch *American Graffiti,* a classic movie about teenage boys who find themselves adrift on their journey to adulthood.

I didn't mention it to my passengers, but I wondered how the sight of your old Nash, with its oxidized, pale blue finish, would support the image of danger and romance we hoped to project. Ferd, who sat next to me in the front seat, passed the jug of peach brandy to me and I took several large gulps. It was sweet-tasting and burned intensely going down my gullet. I drove east on St. Louis Street to Glenstone Avenue, turned around, and drove back to the public square.

We hadn't spotted a single attractive female yet. After another circuit around the public square, I turned north on Boonville Avenue, turned left after a few blocks, and soon we were in front of Springfield's unexpectedly stylish railway station. Passengers traveling through Springfield on a Frisco train must have found it refreshing to discover this station, which was a gem of Southwestern architecture. With its white stuccoed exterior and red tile roof, the rambling, rancho-type structure would have seemed right at home in Santa Fe, New Mexico. But here it was, in the Queen City of the Ozarks.

As we cruised past the Frisco station, I recalled the time Gary Baumberger and I took our dates to dinner at the Harvey House Restaurant there. He and I had indulged in several bourbon-and-Coke highballs, which emboldened us to entertain the girls by stuffing lettuce into our mouths. The waitress had served each of us a lettuce-wedge salad drenched in French dressing. While his date, Doris Reed, and mine, Jo Ann Cassy, nibbled properly at their salads, Gary speared his lettuce wedge with a fork and shoved a corner of it into his mouth. I took up the challenge and followed his example. We both giggled foolishly as we competed to see which one of us could cram the most lettuce into his mouth. We kept at it until we had our mouths around most of the lettuce wedge the waitress had served.

The girls had stopped eating and were staring at us in horror. Saliva began to drip from the corner of my mouth, and I began to feel some panic. My mouth was so full I couldn't chew until the lettuce had dissolved enough to lose mass. I checked to see how Gary was doing and nearly choked. His cheeks were bulging and he, too, was drooling.

Our dates were ignoring us at this point and were having an animated conversation about something else. Gary and I finally excused ourselves and went to the men's room to dispose of our salads.

When I returned to the table, I was exhausted; my jaws ached painfully and my ears were ringing. I was thinking that the girls might say, "Oh, you two! You're soooo funny!" But they didn't. They continued to talk together as if Gary and I didn't exist. I looked at Gary, who grinned ruefully and shrugged. We were young, and we were just beginning to understand that sometimes there's just no accounting for the way women behave.

The memory of that night faded as we drove out of sight of the rail station. The peach brandy was passed around again, and it tasted good. I maneuvered through the sparse Christmas Eve traffic, and eventually, I found that I was near the Southwest

Missouri State College campus. We still had not seen a sign of the four beauties we were seeking.

I drove south on National Avenue; by the time I reached Sunshine Street it was quiet in the car. The fiery peach nectar had made us all thoughtful and reflective. I drove slowly west on Sunshine, feeling warm and giddy. Finally, the silence was broken by Paul, who said, with some difficulty, "At times like these, one wants to be with one's loved ones, doesn't one?"

We all laughed and agreed that yes, one certainly does. Then my riders fell quiet until Paul again broke the silence, this time singing in a strong, nice tenor voice. This is what he sang, to the tune of "Smoke Gets In Your Eyes":

> *They asked me if I knew*
> *raccoon s--t was blue;*
> *I replied and said*
> *you have been misled—*
> *raccoon s--t is red.*

He was rewarded with uproarious laughter. I wanted to reply with another verse, but it needed to be witty and sophisticated because Paul had set a high standard.

While I pondered on rhymes I'd heard, I gazed out the front passenger window and saw that we were passing in front of the highway patrol building west of Springfield. We were almost at the exact spot at which Jimmy Ward had fallen from Ron Gammon's car. He landed on the shoulder of the highway, in full view of any state troopers who might have been staring out their front windows. Fortunately, no trooper was looking, because Ron and Jimmy had been drinking beer in Springfield and wouldn't have had a successful interview with the law officers.

That incident had occurred shortly after I had been sent to the Naval Air Station in Seattle, and the association brought to mind a seafaring rhyme I'd heard a third-class petty officer singing in our barracks. I turned my head slightly and sang it to the tune that introduced *Popeye* cartoons:

> *Tiddly winks, old man,*
> *get a woman if you can—*
> *but if you can't get a woman,*
> *get a clean old man!*

My passengers thought this was very funny, and I continued to think about other bawdy verses I could entertain them with. I recalled some lines you had recited when you felt Bob and I, at age twelve, were old enough to hear them. They were your prescription for proper bathing:

> *Wash as far down as possible.*
> *Then wash as far up as possible.*
> *And then wash possible.*

And I recalled that at about the same age, Bob and I had heard a raunchy couplet from one of the men on the section gang that maintained the tracks on the rail bed that ran through Republic. You would have recognized this one, I'm sure:

> *Cocka-doodle a--hole, my old hen;*
> *she lays eggs for the section men.*
> *Sometimes two and sometimes four;*
> *grease her butt and she'll lay more!*

Well, Jud, I was about to offer the section men's verse when Ferd piped in with a number he'd heard from a college friend. To the tune of "Don't Get Around Much Anymore," he sang these words:

> *Missed the toilet last night,*
> *Went all over the floor,*
> *Wiped it up with a toothbrush,*

Don't brush my teeth much anymore.

We all responded with loud laughter and mock cries of revulsion. Ferd couldn't have been more pleased.

My passengers fell silent after that. From my driver's-side window I saw on the left a barn and smaller buildings that were part of Emmett Roberts's farm. During the months that I worked at Union National Bank in Springfield, I had sometimes driven up the dirt lane to give Mr. Roberts a ride to Springfield. He returned the favor by helping me buy gasoline for my Plymouth. During our drives to and from Springfield, we made small talk and he would tell me stories and verses from his youth—one of which began to form in my mind as I drove along. When all of the words came to me, I decided that it would do. I turned my head again and repeated Mr. Roberts's rhyme:

> *When the weather's hot and sultry,*
> *that's no time for adultery.*
> *But when the frost is on the pumpkin,*
> *that's the time for peter-dunkin'.*

I couldn't have chosen a better selection. Even Paul the urbane thrashed about in the back seat, shrieking his appreciation. But, soon, the brandy began to take hold again, and my passengers grew quiet. I was concerned because Paul and Ferd seemed to be dozing, and the night was still young.

After some minutes of silence, Josh, my front-seat passenger who had offered nothing during the evening, began to sing in a small, sweet voice:

> *Oh, it's going to be a long, long winter;*
> *and what will the birdies do then,*
> *the poor things?*
> *They'll fly to the barn*
> *to keep themselves warm,*

> *and tuck their heads under their wings,*
> *the poor things.*

There was no response from the rear seat, and from the corner of my eye I could see Josh sitting self-consciously, staring straight ahead. After a moment, he said to no one in particular, "My sister learned that at Girl Scout camp."

I felt that someone needed to respond, so I said, "That was nice." I decided that the evening was deteriorating badly, and that some strong coffee might energize us all.

We were now approaching the *Y* where Highway 174 joins Highway 60, so I veered to the right and drove on 174 toward Suggs' Truck Stop and Café. It wasn't quite nine o'clock when I parked in front of the café. We all filed sleepily inside for our coffee.

When we came outside again, we saw Clarence Cottrell leaning against the front of the café. He was standing there with his back against the wall and seemed to be staring at the gravel on the parking area. When we spoke to him, he didn't reply, and we discovered that he was asleep. Just standing there, asleep. At that moment, with his back still flat against the building, he began to slide toward the ground. Clarence slid very slowly, as if he were a thick glob of something that someone had thrown against the wall.

It was very cold outside, and Clarence obviously had been drinking. We helped him to his feet and wrestled him into the back of the Nash. Ferd and Paul weren't pleased, because the backseat really wasn't wide enough for three people to be comfortable. Clarence didn't object, and the ride to his house would be short enough that Ferd and Paul wouldn't be discommoded for more than a few minutes. In any case, Jud, we had no choice. Clarence might have fallen down and frozen if he had tried to get home under his own locomotion.

I drove south on Main Street and turned into Clarence's neighborhood near the water tower. He began to mumble his profound thanks as I stopped in front of his house.

We helped Clarence exit the car, and he seemed able to stand by himself. When I told him he was home, he raised his eyebrows in an effort to get his eyes open. He then attempted a courtly bow, which caused him to stumble forward slightly. We turned him around, aimed him at the house, and let him go. Josh started to take Clarence's arm and help him walk, but Ferd signaled to let him go on alone. I guess we all wanted to see how far he'd make it on his own.

Clarence began the long trek to the front door, which was barely visible in the moonlight. He stepped forward for several feet, then veered sharply to the right. He made a large, wobbly circle across the damp grass and headed back in our direction. But before he reached the car, his feet made another turn, and he was off again in the general direction of the house.

Clarence's legs were becoming less and less reliable. He weaved and leaned crazily, but he managed to stay on the sidewalk this time. Halfway to the porch, he stopped and faced the house, swaying. After he had steadied himself, he raised both arms and extended them forward, palms together in a diving pose. He seemed to be using his upright thumbs to sight on the front door. Still holding his arms in this position, he staggered forward and disappeared into the darkness of the porch. I heard a loud crash, followed by thrashing, scuffing noises as Clarence apparently struggled to regain his footing. Lights went on inside the house, and when the front door opened slightly, some of the light spilled onto the porch.

A woman's voice said, "Clarence? Clarence?"

It was time for us to leave, so we climbed into the Nash and I started the engine. As we drove away, Ferd cranked down his window and shouted, "Merry Christmas!"

I could hear the woman's voice saying, "What? What?"

Everyone was ready to go home by this time, and I began the drive to Springfield. I felt disconsolate. My big night out with the sophisticates had been a bust. We had not found romance or any adventure that we could brag about later. Instead, we had been reduced to drinking like amateurs and shouting vulgar rhymes to entertain ourselves.

Furthermore, the logistics of our evening had been poorly planned. I had brought my friends home to Republic, yet their cars were still parked in Springfield. I said very little during the drive back to Springfield, which was just as well since my passengers all seemed comatose.

After I said goodbye to my sleepy friends, I drove the Nash toward the highway again for the return trip to Republic, thinking that it felt nothing at all like Christmas Eve. I felt empty and depressed. My vague expectations of the evening had never materialized and there would be no holiday adventures for me to share when I returned to Seattle.

On that late Christmas Eve, while you and Isabel slept, I cracked my side window to let the cold air blow against my face, and I remembered another of Emmett Roberts's favorite Depression-era sentiments:

> *If we had some ham,*
> *we could have ham and eggs,*
> *if we had some eggs.*

Don

Dear Jud:

Mack Doyle was the first person I told about my new job at Lynn and Irene Martin's Republic Theater. I was already working at Western Auto that summer and Mack came in to look at some open-end wrenches. While I was ringing up the sale, I mentioned that I was going to start working at night as the projectionist and that Truman Cook was going to teach me how to run the projectors. I was expecting some congratulations, but all Mack offered was "True Cook? He's got twelve fangers," as if that bit of news might be a deal breaker.

I had never given much thought to what True did to make the Friday night double feature appear on the movie house screen. But I had noticed that he had more than a full set of fingers while watching him eat a hamburger at the Republic Café.

None of that was on my mind the night you told me about the opening at the Republic Theater. You said that True had accepted another job and that Lynn, who was looking for a replacement, asked if you thought I would be interested. Lynn had told you that True could train me how to run the movie projectors in about a week's time.

Since I was already working at Western Auto that summer between my junior and senior years at high school, my first reaction to this offer was negative. A nighttime movie job would bring to an end my carefree summer evenings. But, as is so often the case, money decided it. I was making $10 a week in my day job at Western Auto, and running the projectors at night would double my income. Also, the idea of working with those machines began to intrigue me. The possibility of earning $20 every week—pretty good money in 1950—was compelling. So I went to see Lynn the following day. He hired me right away, and I became a motion picture operator, taught by a man who may have been the only twelve-fingered movie projectionist in America.

In *Cinema Paradiso,* a wonderfully touching Italian film you'd have enjoyed, a young boy, Salvatore, has an unhappy life with his indifferent parents. He finds refuge in the projection booth of his Sicilian village's movie house. There, he forms a bond with the grumpy old projectionist, Alfredo, who inspires in Salvatore a love for moviemaking. Salvatore eventually goes on to become a famous film director in Rome.

True's influence on me wasn't quite that profound. But he welcomed me warmly when I entered the Republic Theater's dingy little projection booth that first night, and I found him to be a patient, good-natured teacher. Even so, on that first night I thought I would never be able to master all of the tasks that True showed me. To run the picture show, I would be required to check the film, load it into the projectors, load the carbon arc lamp house with pencil-sized sticks of carbon, throw the electrical switch that fired the powerful arc lights, adjust the automatic carbon feed, keep the film in focus, and, when the dots appeared in the upper right corner of the image on the theater screen, make a smooth changeover from one projector to the other.

True usually kept a lighted cigarette clamped between his lips, in the center of his mouth, right under his nose. I watched the smoke curl up into his eyes, making him squint as he showed me how to thread the wide ribbon of 35 mm film into one of the Simplex projectors. Small doors opened to reveal the machine's two film compartments, which were small and cramped and full of sprocket wheels and other metal components made hot by the projector's arc light. Having an extra finger on each hand didn't make it any easier for True to loop the film around the sprocket wheels and through the film gate. Cigarette still clenched between his lips, he'd mutter "Yod-yam it!" when he snagged one of the extra fingers on a sharp-toothed sprocket. The fingers were non-functional little appendages that stuck out like dew claws on a dog's ankle. He noticed that I was watching, and he grinned at me through the blue haze of cigarette smoke. "One of these days," he said, "I'm gonna have to cut them yod-yam fingers off!"

By the end of that first night in the projection booth I was still apprehensive but I knew I was going to love the job. I liked the heat and the brilliance of the electric arc lamps. The odor of the blazing rods of carbon made me think of the "ozone" Isabel claimed she could smell in the air on certain summer days. I liked the steady clattering of the film as it snapped through the film gate. And, especially, I liked the feeling of power I felt when I peered through the projection booth's portholes at the shadowy forms of the moviegoers below, knowing that I was going to be in charge of the shows they'd be coming to see.

It was late when I finally got home that night after helping True rewind the film and clean and oil the projectors, but I was too energized to go to sleep. I lay in the dark and thought about those two big projection machines, and I felt a shiver in my stomach at the realization that I'd soon be operating them by myself.

Before I knew it, True had spent his final night in the booth, and he was gone. I was on my own. The following evening, I reported for duty as the Republic Theater's official projectionist. Dixie Carter was getting her popcorn machine ready as I began my climb up to the projection room. Lynn leaned out of the ticket booth and said, "Are you ready, buddy?" I nodded, confidently, I thought. But he must have seen the look on my face, because he said, "Don't worry, Don. True said you'd do fine. And if there's a problem, I'm always right here."

I got through my solo performance that night without incident and got a thumbs-up from Lynn at the end of the evening. On the following night, I again projected the movie flawlessly, and for the next ten days or so, I performed so well that Lynn said I was a natural projectionist. I took this praise to heart, and I began to think about becoming a motion picture operator at one of the big movie houses in Springfield.

My success was an intoxicating experience, made even more so by the appearance of Ann, Irene's pretty niece from Tulsa. I remembered her from her annual summer visits with Irene's parents, the Craigs. Mr. Craig had been one of my yard-mowing customers, and Ann was the shy adolescent girl who had brought tall, icy-cold glasses of lemonade to sustain me as I worked in the hot sun.

One evening, as I was splicing film for the *Previews of Coming Attractions* reel, I heard a tap at the door. When I opened it, I saw a slender, dark-haired girl, and, after a moment, I recognized Ann's pale-blue eyes. I guess I just stood there with my mouth open, because she smiled and asked if she could watch me operate the projectors. The crisp cotton dress she wore rustled as she stepped into the booth. I detected a slightly proprietary air about the way she walked directly to the stool by my workbench. She sat on the stool, crossed her legs, clasped her hands over a knee, and gazed wide-eyed around the room. "You know how to run all this stuff?" she asked.

I said I did in an offhand manner that I hoped would imply easy familiarity, and I started the show. I tried to go about my tasks casually but knowing that a tanned, long-legged, pretty female was watching every move made concentration difficult. Somehow, I made it through the previews, cartoon, and feature film without any mistakes. She stayed in the booth until the movie was over and I had finished my cleaning and shutdown routine. We were the last people to leave the theater, so I locked the door and offered to walk her home. Thus began a pattern that was repeated several times a week that summer. Ann would join me in the projection booth, and, after the movie, we'd walk together in the peaceful darkness of Elm Street. When we reached the Craigs' house, we'd sit together on the porch swing listening to the night sounds and talking quietly about our interests. It was a summer romance, but I was too shy to try to kiss her—especially since I was pretty sure that on one occasion, at least, I had seen Mr. Craig's shadowy form standing on the other side of the front screen door.

My skill as a projectionist continued to improve that summer, for a while. Then—and I don't know whether it was from overconfidence or the distraction of a pretty female companion—things suddenly began to go wrong.

I'd forget to check the length of the carbon rods in the lamp house, and the arc light would burn out in mid-reel. I failed to lock a reel on the rewind spindle, and, just as the unwinding reel reached maximum speed, it came off the spindle, skidded on the metal surface of my workbench and, mimicking a scene from one of the cartoons I'd shown, gained traction and launched itself against the wall on the right side of the small room—where it rebounded and shot past my head to career off the wall on the left side of the booth. By this time, I was on the floor with my arms over my head. I could hear the runaway reel bouncing and clattering against the film cans near me. I also heard Lynn's voice coming from below.

"Don? Everything okay up there?"

"Yep," I replied, hoping to sound unconcerned.

"Good," said Lynn's voice. "Sounded like you were doing some remodeling."

Several nights later I made another error that produced hoots and catcalls from the darkened theater below me. Before showtime, when I checked the film for *The Boy With Green Hair,* starring Dean Stockwell, it appeared to me that the second reel of the movie hadn't been rewound from the previous showing (I soon found out that it had been). So, I rewound it in the usual fashion. At 7:30 PM, I started the movie. All went well through the previews, cartoon, and first reel of the feature film. When I hit the changeover buttons to switch to reel number two, the boy with green hair appeared on the screen upside-down, and the film's optical sound track was visible as a jagged vertical bar on the right side of the screen. There was nothing for me to do but stop the movie and turn on the auditorium lights. Lynn appeared in the projection booth and asked me what happened.

I said, "I think someone rewound that reel wrong."

He said, "I think so, too," and gave me a meaningful look. He checked the rewound film to make sure I'd done it right this time and left the booth while I re-threaded the projector and restarted the movie. I was glad that he and Irene had already gone home when I climbed down the ladder at the end of that evening.

You might have thought that I couldn't have created a situation more humiliating than that, but you'd have been wrong. It was a Friday night, the night when my peers were most likely to be in attendance because, for the low ticket price of twenty-five cents, we treated our patrons to a newsreel, a western movie, previews of coming attractions, a serial episode, and another feature film—usually a *B* picture murder mystery.

As usual, I arrived well before showtime to haul the heavy film cans up the ladder and into the projection booth. The Warner Pathe News and other short subjects came to us on small reels, so, for the sake of expedience, I spliced the newsreel and serial episode together and wound them on one reel. After checking the feature films, I placed all of the reels in vertical bins so that they would be ready and in the order that I needed them: previews, cowboy movie (which that night was a Gene Autry film), newsreel and serial, then the second feature.

During the sorting process, I had managed to transpose the second reel of the Gene Autry movie with the reel that held the Warner Pathe News. I then threaded both projectors and, at the appointed time, began the movie. As the first reel of the western movie ended, I pressed the changeover buttons to switch to the second reel. The result was electrifying. The first reel had ended with Gene astride Champion, singing a song as he rode along a scenic desert trail. That pastoral scene was abruptly replaced by the thrilling image of a huge black-hulled ocean freighter smashing into to the dock of some eastern seaport. Through the projection room porthole I could see taunting faces in the audience turned my way, and I could hear the jeering over the soundtrack.

I'm convinced that I kept my position only because there was no other projectionist in town, other than Lynn, and he just didn't want to start all over again, training a new one. So I survived that series of mishaps and, motivated by fear and pride, I applied myself the way you seemed to in your railroad work. From that point on, I used extra care to check the film reels, I made sure the lamp houses held sufficient carbon, and I practiced making seamless changeovers. Soon, I was back in Lynn's good graces.

Something else also happened. Between changeovers, after I had prepared the alternate projector and had little to do but watch the movie, I began to think about what had taken place when I became Republic's motion picture operator. The realization was an epiphany: for the first time in my life I was involved in an *occupation*—not just another odd job. I could envision my future as a projectionist, perhaps in Springfield, perhaps at the prestigious Gilloiz Theater on St. Louis street, or the Electric Theater on the public square. No more farmhand jobs for me!

* * * * * * * * * * *

At the time, I would never have admitted to you or Isabel that I didn't hate every odd job that came my way. But I can say it now: in several instances the working conditions were bizarre enough, or the behavior of the employer was quirky and eccentric enough, that Bob or I might have taken on the job for no pay.

For example, how many people can list "gravedigger" as a previous occupation on their resume? I could, although it would be stretching the facts to some extent. When Uncle Bob Thurman called to see if Bob and I could handle a project for him, we quickly accepted for the sheer novelty of the assignment.

It was a special situation. The remains of a woman who had been buried in another state for many years had been transferred to Uncle Bob's funeral home in Republic for re-interment in Evergreen Cemetery. Since her remains were much reduced and wouldn't require the space provided by a full-sized casket, Uncle Bob didn't see any reason to hire his regular gravedigger to dig a regulation six-foot-deep grave.

As I recall, Bob took the call from Uncle Bob, who described the small project he had. We were intrigued, discussed it, and agreed to do it. That's how we became the only people I know (outside of the cemetery business) who are able (or willing) to say they have dug a grave and buried a body in it.

We met Uncle Bob at the cemetery and followed the big, black hearse along one of the gravel drives until we reached the spot where we were to dig the grave. We unloaded the small coffin and gently placed it on the grass nearby. We then dug a hole according to Uncle Bob's specifications. When we reached the specified depth, we picked up the coffin, which was surprisingly light since not much of the deceased's remains remained, lowered it into the ground and replaced the soil.

Compared with farm labor, this was an easy job, and we might have offered to work as gravediggers again if the regular digger hadn't threatened us with his shovel.

You always seemed to enjoy my impressions of Gerald Wainright's telephone messages after he would call to secure my services as a chauffeur. After one of those calls, I could hardly wait to see you so that I could mimic Gerald's adenoidal whine and odd speech pattern. Although I ridiculed his calls, I looked forward to them since they represented easy work and generous pay.

When Gerald's mother felt too weak to drive their automobile on shopping expeditions, she would ask him to hire me to drive them to Springfield or some other destination. I was always fascinated by Gerald's complex speaking habits. At the end of each phrase or sentence, he would clear his throat with a "hmmm!" and repeat the last syllable or two of the last word in the sentence. It sounded something like this:

"Hello, Don ... hmmm! ... on? This is Gerald Wainright ... hmmm! ... ainright. How are you ... hmmm! ... oo? My mother was wondering ... hmmm! ... undering ... if you could drive us to Springfield ... hmmm! ... eengfield ... in the morning ...

hmmm! … orning. You can … hmmm! … ann? Good … hmmm! … ood. We'll see you tomorrow … hmmm! … orrow."

It's hard to imagine how Gerald might have proposed to a girl, but if he did, I sure would like to have been listening.

You knew Carl Price as a man who sat serenely during services at Hood Methodist, and you were shocked to hear about his behavior the morning he hired me to help him haul hay. His conduct that morning shocked me, too, at first. But, after I recovered, I was able to regale all my friends with a vivid account of that experience, which remains one of my favorite memories of Republic.

I had always hated hauling hay, but when Carl hired me, he said it was just a small field and that we'd be finished before noon. So I reported to his farm in relatively good spirits.

My job was to walk behind Carl, who was towing a flatbed wagon with his tractor, and hoist bails of hay onto the wagon. The tractor engine had been acting up, he said. At mid-morning, it made a huge, hollow, coughing noise and lurched forward violently several times. Carl flopped around on the bucking tractor, hanging on for dear life. When the cantankerous engine stopped and all was silent, Carl leaped from his seat and ran to the front of the machine. He glared at its headlights and screamed "You dirty sonofabitch!" He then stooped, grabbed a large rock, and hurled it, banging it off the tractor hood. "Goddamn you, you bastard!" He found another rock and threw it into the engine compartment. "Rotten sonofabitch!"

Carl stared at the tractor, panting, and then he turned to me. "You may as well go on home now, Don," he said quietly. I was glad to go. I didn't ask him for any pay, because I really didn't care about that. What I had witnessed was rewarding enough. And it confirmed my intention to look for job opportunities away from the farm.

It was not long after that day that the opportunity I couldn't have dreamed of materialized: Lynn Martin's offer to hire me as Republic's movie projectionist.

The job itself and the money I earned were so dear to me that, when my senior year of high school began that fall, I decided to continue working at night at the theater. This meant I'd have to quit being a member of the high school's basketball team. Coach McMurtry wasn't happy when we discussed my plans and tried to persuade me to stay with the team. But the appeal of my movie job was too strong, and I quit the team.

I know that you had some mixed feelings about that decision, since I'd probably have been one of the starting five in my senior year. But in the end, it was a good decision because the experience I gained proved to be a useful and valuable asset. Within a couple of years, I was called to active duty in the U.S. Naval Reserve, and shortly after I reported to Sand Point Naval Air Station in Seattle, I found that the recreation department was looking for an additional person to rotate among the projectionists at the base's movie theater. I applied, was accepted, and was sent to the U.S. Naval School for Motion Picture Protectionists in San Diego, California, for training that I really didn't need. But the training certificate was a requirement, so I went.

The experience at our base theater served me well after I was released from active duty in the summer of 1956. With my military service requirement behind me, Phyl and George invited me to stay with them while I investigated the possibility of attending Texas Tech University in Lubbock, Texas. That move was the reason for the departure I described in my first letter. Once in Lubbock, I was hired as one of two projectionists needed to operate the machines at the Golden Horseshoe Drive-In Theater—a spectacular new drive-in movie at the end of town. I'll recall that time only enough to say that I didn't attend Texas Tech, I didn't remain in Lubbock, and I didn't pursue a career as a movie projectionist after that since I had decided to become a dentist—another career that I ultimately didn't pursue.

I still feel a vague stirring when I walk up the aisle of a movie theater and glance upward to the windows of the projection booth. Perhaps I inherited the dreamer in you, and it was the dreamer in me that made showing movies so appealing. I know how much you enjoyed watching films, and I suspect you could lose yourself in the stories on the screen the way I always have. I saw that aspect of you the night in 1951 on which we braved an ice storm to drive ten miles over nearly impassable roads to see the film adaptation of Jacques Offenbach's opera, *The Tales of Hoffman.*

The streets and highways throughout Greene County were glazed with ice, and Isabel told us we were crazy to even try driving to the Plaza Theater in Springfield, where the film was showing. But you said you were game if I was, and so we set out. You said I should drive since my reflexes were probably better than yours. I began our trip by heading slowly down Elm Street toward town so that I could take Main Street to Highway 174, and then on to Springfield. It would have been shorter to drive east on Elm Street to Highway 60, but I feared I might lose control on the iced-over incline where Elm crossed the highway. As it happened, I lost control anyway. When we reached the Elm and Main intersection, my foot touched the brake pedal just enough to slow us for the turn, but that light tap sent us into a slow-motion spin, a graceful pirouette that left us facing the way we'd come. The maneuver rendered you nearly helpless with laughter, and you shook your head at the folly of our adventure. But we proceeded and eventually made it to Springfield, seeing only one or two other motorists foolish enough to be driving on the iced roads that night.

We made it to our seats in the Plaza Theater in time for the beginning of *The Tales of Hoffman*, and we were soon absorbed in the magical fantasy of this film version of the opera. When I glanced at you, as I did when Moira Shearer performed as Olympia, the ballerina doll, and again during the brooding scenes of Venice accompanied by the haunting "Barcarolle," you were gazing at the screen with such rapt wonder that I knew you were as glad we had made the trip as I was.

I have enjoyed the career I eventually settled upon. It has enabled me to meet people I've been privileged to know and to see parts of the world I otherwise might never have seen. Yet when I recall my evenings beside those machines, revive the smell of the lamp houses, and hear again the thrumming of film through the film gates, I think that I have seldom been happier at work than I was when confined for those hours in my projection booth.

Don

The day is done, and the darkness
Falls from the wings of night,
As a feather is wafted downward
from an eagle in his flight.
            —Henry Wadsworth Longfellow

Dear Jud:

I wasn't prepared for the emotions I felt that day I drove into Republic and discovered that your depot was gone. On my previous trips back to Republic, I had developed a "coming home" ritual: I would leave Interstate 44 at the Highway N exit, turn right on Highway N, and drive south toward Republic. The old warm excitement always stirred in my stomach when I began to see familiar barns and farmhouses, and, when the highway became North Main Street, I'd nearly sprain my neck gazing at both sides of the street to see houses that seemed to change little over the years.

When I reached the point where the railroad tracks crossed Main, I would always glance to the right for a reassuring look at the depot—the official emblem of my return home. But on this trip, the distinctive gray and white structure that I identified so closely with you, the dusty, drafty old building that was such an integral part of your life—of the lives of us all—was simply gone.

I suppose I shouldn't have been surprised. Republic's downtown blocks had undergone changes, and most of the business establishments I'd known were gone, too—the result of the "Wal-Martization" of small-town America.

You, yourself, had been gone for more than fifteen years before I found the depot vanished. Yet when I gazed at the weedy, graveled space where your depot had stood, I felt an almost physical sensation, a gentle parting of the last, fragile filament that had connected me to your time here.

I pulled my car onto the gravel of the depot's former parking area, got out, and walked to a point beside the main line tracks. The creosote odor from the railroad ties was familiar and good. I turned northward to look past the now vacant depot property, and, across West Elm Street, I could see what was once the showroom and service area of French Chevrolet. Republic's Chevrolet and Ford dealerships were no longer located downtown. They had moved to the new shopping district on Highway 60, which was becoming one of those franchise and fast-food clusters that seem to appear at the edge of every town and city in America.

I brought my gaze back and tried to estimate the location of the depot waiting room door. I could almost see that old room where Bob and I had spent so many hours. Moving forward several yards, I imagined that I was stepping through the doorway. I paused for a moment and thought about the day Bob and I rolled our new bicycles into this room and began to ride in a wild, erratic circle. Dust rose into the air as we sped around the room, barely missing the potbelly stove and the benches that lined the walls.

I tried to visualize the clunky old gum machine that had hung on the wall next to your ticket window. When Bob and I had a penny to spend, we'd drop it in the coin slot, pull one of the levers beneath the four rows of chewing gum the machine offered, and pluck our purchases from the bottom of the machine. Our choices included Dentyne, Beeman's Pepsin (my favorite), and Chiclets Peppermint or Spearmint, which came in tiny boxes containing two small pillows of gum.

I could picture the patriotic posters that had adorned the walls during World War II. My favorite was the one with the picture of Uncle Sam, who pointed at us and commanded us to buy U.S. War Bonds. Another one warned, ominously—and irrelevantly, considering that we lived nearly a thousand miles from the nearest ocean water—that "Loose Lips Sink Ships!"

During the early war years, it had made me uneasy to think that there might be German or Japanese spies in Republic. When I asked if you thought there were spies among us, your answer was a conspiratorial, "You never know." That didn't ease my mind, and I began to wonder if anyone we knew kept a shortwave radio in the attic. I visualized a shadowy figure in the dim light of an attic, mouth pressed against a microphone, passing along important details about the trainloads of tanks and cannons that passed through town. At night, when you slipped on your Civil Defense armband and set out to stroll Republic's dark streets looking for violators of the blackout drills, I hoped that you might come across a spy and apprehend him or her.

Now, standing in the gravel a few yards from where the depot's bay windows once were, I thought about your view from that position when you were tapping out messages on the railroad telegraph. From your perspective there, approaching trains seemed to be headed directly for you. But you sat there at your desk, unperturbed, knowing that the tracks would lead the roaring engines safely past you.

Those two large levers that rose vertically through slots in your desk top always drew me to that bay-window desk, especially when Bob and I rode our bikes to the depot and we found you seated at one of your other desks. We usually argued over whose turn it was to sit in the bay-window chair and operate the semaphore signals that the levers controlled. You kept the levers locked, so we could only pretend we were moving them.

At that age, I believed I had special qualifications to operate and maintain the semaphores, which were used to send signals to approaching trains since the locomotives weren't equipped with radios in the 1940s. This belief was based on my ability to climb trees and telephone poles. Isabel had said that, due to the way I could scamper about in the three ash trees in front of our house, she felt I must be part monkey. I took the compliment literally, and thereafter I began to assess the amount of hair on my arms and legs to see if I was becoming any more monkey-like.

It was after I had acquired this new sense of my monkey-ness that I stood watching you one morning as you cautiously made your way up the rickety ladder on the semaphore tower that stood outside your depot window. You were climbing up the twenty-foot tower to change one of the light bulbs that illuminated the red and green semaphore paddles. Watching you, I knew I could have scrambled to the top of the tower in a fraction of the time it was taking you. When you returned to solid ground, I mentioned my qualifications and applied for the job. You could have dismissed me by saying it was too dangerous for a young boy. Instead, you explained that we would have to send my application to Frisco headquarters and that you were pretty sure they wouldn't accept it until I was eighteen years old. Jud, at that moment it came to me—I believe for the first time—that you didn't make all the rules about what went on at the depot, that the Frisco Railroad made the really big rules. The realization that I would have to wait another ten years to send in my semaphore tower-climbing application disappointed me. But I remember feeling good that my age disqualification came from Frisco instead of you.

You weren't nearly so diplomatic when you disallowed our help placing those signal torpedoes on the big main line track. You said they weren't like Fourth of July fireworks. These were powerful explosives, you said, and they could blow our hands off. The torpedoes were lethal-looking packages shaped like reddish little pillows made of waxy cardboard. Lead straps extended from each side of the torpedo so that when you placed one on top of the rail, you could secure it in place by bending the lead straps under the lips of the rail. You explained to us that, by spacing the torpedoes apart at certain intervals, you could send a code message to the locomotive crew, who would hear the loud reports as the heavy engine wheels smashed the torpedoes and caused them to explode.

I always wondered what would happen if I laid one of the gunpowder packages on our front sidewalk and pounded it with a hammer. I can say now, as I type with two hands, I'm glad I never had that opportunity.

Isabel told us she hated it when you had to stand close to the tracks and lift paper messages up to the engineers as they sped by. If we happened to be at the depot when you needed to communicate this way, we could watch you type out a message, fold it and attach it to a special length of twine, which you strung between the *Y* arms at the end of a long pole. I would imagine what it would be like to walk to within a few feet of the main line tracks, as you did, and hold the pole toward the locomotive that was speeding toward us at forty or fifty miles an hour. I admired the nerve of the crewman who would stand in the door of the cab, lean out as far as he could, and snatch the message from the pole by hooking it in the crook of his arm. At that moment of contact, you always leaned to the left and did a funny little dance in the gravel to keep your balance.

Railroad people communicate with locomotive crews by radio today. I doubt if any of them ever have romantic notions of doing it the way you did.

It was chilly the afternoon I stood by the tracks and faced the weedy rectangle that was the only trace of the train station that once had stood there. I hunched my shoulders against the cold breeze, and, looking to my right, I saw two women standing at the rear of an automobile parked diagonally on Main Street. They were staring at me. Perhaps they were wondering why a stranger would stand alone at that spot. I waved an arm and said, "Afternoon, ladies. Where did the depot go?" They quickly opened the vehicle's trunk, dumped their packages in it, and got into the car. I wondered what they were saying to each other as they drove away, heading north on Main.

They might not have lived in Republic long enough to remember the depot. If they had, they may have recalled it vaguely as a long, gray landmark, a place of little importance that had fallen into disuse and sat empty for a year or so before it was demolished. I wince at that word, which denotes crashing and splintering. It is a brutal word when used in connection with your depot.

The building had been there all through my growing-up years, and it seemed to have always been there. I was surprised when I learned that it wasn't the first depot to occupy that site. You never spoke of it, so I wonder if you had known about the first depot, since it had been built and then torn down before your time. If not, here's a bit of depot history:

According to a book on Republic's history that I obtained a number of years ago, the first rail line through the settlement now called Republic was completed in 1870. The history book recounts how members of the community contacted the railroad company (then called the South Pacific Railroad) and asked for a switching station and depot. The railroad apparently wasn't interested in the proposition, so the citizens passed the hat and raised $1,000. That was enough to build a pretty good country depot in those days—a hundred years before the day I stood on the empty depot property.

You were nine years old when the railroad company became interested in Republic and replaced the original structure with a permanent depot, which was called Station 252, Republic, Missouri. That was in 1898. When you became the stationmaster in 1933, the building was thirty-five years old and had been expanded over the years. The waiting room had been made larger and an express room had been added to the freight and baggage room.

By the time you took over, Frisco's passenger business was already dwindling. Fewer passenger trains stopped at Republic because people had begun to travel more and more by bus or automobile. Even Frisco had begun to operate a bus line to compete with the other bus companies, such as Greyhound and Trailways, that served southwest Missouri. I can remember watching you at your ticket window as you sold Frisco bus tickets to Springfield,

Aurora, Monett—even to Billings, which was only four miles from Republic (near enough for a not-too-tiring walk).

The gravel "floor" of the waiting room was making my feet cold, so I turned to my left and stepped forward through another imaginary door into the space your office had occupied. The warm and dusty-sweet office smell flooded my nose as I walked through the weeds and gravel to what might have been remnants of the freight room's heavy plank flooring.

Once, thirty years earlier, I could have turned right and entered the small, evil-smelling storage closet where you kept your torpedoes, flares, and other exotic supplies. I almost felt the raspy catch in the throat produced by breathing the air in that little room. I visualized the grimy boxes where you kept the blue vitriol rocks and the odd-looking zinc elements from which Bob and I made the storage batteries that powered your telegraph equipment. This was one of our favorite depot projects.

You'd disconnect the batteries, which looked like large glass jars filled with dirty water and gravel, from your telegraph equipment. We'd then pour out the water and remove the spent blue vitriol (you called it "vitrel") and the zinc "crow's foot." You called the zinc element that because it resembled the leg and three-toed foot of a huge bird. Next, we'd place a fresh crow's foot in the glass container, fill the container about half full of blue vitriol, and pour in fresh water. After a time, the reaction of these chemicals and water would produce a mild electrical current—not enough to tingle our fingers, but enough to make your telegraph chatter.

I spotted a dark mass among the weeds several feet from where I stood. I walked over and kicked it, splintering the edge of a heavy plank whose age-blackened surface barely protruded above the rocky soil. I guessed that it was a plank from the freight room's elevated loading platform, and an unpleasant memory came to me.

I had come to the depot to visit you one afternoon and found you on the freight platform, struggling to load a heavy carton onto your dolly. Joe, the freight truck driver, was leaning on a crate, watching indifferently. It was hot in the freight room, and your face was red and sweat was dripping from your nose and chin.

I looked at Joe, who watched you toil the way I might have watched an ant, and I could feel anger boiling. Most of what passed through the freight room were relatively small cartons headed for the merchants on main street. But some of the cartons were huge and heavy, and stood as tall as I was. It was one of those that you were struggling with that afternoon.

Isabel often told Bob and me about the heart trouble that ran in our family; *both* sides, she emphasized. This caused me to believe that I was dying every time I had gas pains in my chest. I thought about your condition—the heart murmur that had kept you out of World War I. And I looked at Joe, leaning casually against the crate, chomping furiously on his chewing gum. I glared at his thick, trunk-like body and his startlingly homely face. Someone had broken his nose so that the bridge now nestled nearly flat against his face and only the fleshy nostril part protruded. But it was his chin that bothered me most. It was huge, extending forward and upward so far that when he chewed his gum, as he was doing, chin and nose-tip nearly touched.

You were still straining, red-faced and panting, with the carton. And at that moment, I had a violent fantasy. I saw myself delivering a stinging left jab to Joe's nose, followed by a thunderous right hook to the chin, sending him staggering backwards into a pile of heavy packages which came crashing down upon him.

I wasn't able to do that, of course, but I did go home and tell Isabel, whose famous temper flared. She said that if she'd been there, "that man wouldn't have been leaning against his damned dolly!" If you got an earful that night, it was my fault.

I allowed that bittersweet reverie to fade as I walked across the freight room site toward the spot where, once, a heavy sliding door opened to the outdoor loading area by the tracks. I stepped through that imagined space and strolled to the main line tracks. Those same tracks might have been in place since before the depot had been torn down. But they weren't Frisco tracks anymore, and, as I looked at them, I no longer had that faintly proprietary sense that they were "our" tracks.

It may sound odd that railroad tracks could look alien, but these did to me. The trains that rode on these sturdy, silvery parallel bars were no longer owned by Frisco. The Burlington Northern Railroad Company had acquired the St. Louis–San Francisco Railway, and the trains that now ran through Republic were Burlington Northern trains.

That all came about after you had gone, and that's probably the way it was supposed to be. You were a Frisco man for fifty years, and I don't believe you'd have wanted to be associated with the new name and the new way of doing business.

Standing there, I noticed that it was getting cooler and the daylight was fading rapidly. I checked my watch and saw that it was nearly five o'clock. On a September evening perhaps fifteen years earlier, you might have been tidying the stacks of unprocessed papers that you'd tackle again the following morning. Soon after that, you'd have flipped off the office light switch and made your way through the darkened, and still empty, waiting room.

With the door locked behind you, you'd have stepped carefully over the tracks to begin your walk home, turning onto Elm at the library building. The weathered brick sidewalk would lead you past the O'Neal Lumber & Coal Company storage yard, where, perhaps, you'd take a deep breath to refresh your nose, as we so often did, with the sharp, pungent fragrance of wet, raw lumber. And at that point, you might step upon the ancient concrete patch that bore the faint impression of the extended-finger greeting I had left there long ago (still sleazy after all these years).

Now, your legs would settle into that familiar cadence, carrying you steadily past the pleasant homes and the tall trees that created dappled sun patterns along Elm Street in the summer and waved stark branches on breezy winter evenings.

Your ten-minute stroll would bring you to our front sidewalk and you'd be home again after another long day of railroad work. Another rewarding evening would await: a warm supper, conversation with Isabel, a pipe or two beside your beloved old radio.

When the evening was over, you'd settle into bed, say goodnight to Isabel, and close your eyes. During the night, Isabel would hear you sigh and she would go back to sleep, not knowing until the morning that you'd drifted into the deep and peaceful sleep that concluded the good life you had lived.

* * * * * * * * * *

When I was a boy, I sometimes wished that Bob and I could have gone hunting with you, as some of our friends did with their fathers. I wondered at times why you never took us fishing or simply accompanied us on our hikes through the fields surrounding Republic. The reason you didn't, I suspect, had more to do with age and experience than with inclination. I never heard you speak of taking part in those activities with your father, who apparently never shared with you the experience of hunting, fishing, or hiking.

You were a middle-aged man when we were born, and, as we grew older, so did you. Your physical condition and the demands of your long hours at the depot frequently left you too tired at the end of the day to do much more than putter in the garden for a while or to just sit on the front porch.

But you managed to spend good times with us, and I'm grateful for what I did learn from you. You taught me how to use a hammer, how to saw a straight line across a board, and how to make things with my hands. From you I learned how to be an observer and to remember what I observed. In what spare time you had, you took Bob and me to watch a big-league baseball game in St. Louis. You rode with us in a pickup truck to purchase new bicycles in Crane, Missouri. In 1942 you took us to the old Springfield municipal airport to see the new Boeing B-17 bomber that had flown into Springfield on a public relations tour.

I can still see it gleaming silver on the airport apron, with bold red and white stripes painted on its rudder. And I remember the excitement of crawling through the bomber's cramped fuselage when the crew let the three of us see what the aircraft looked like inside.

When Bob and I were performing, you and Isabel never missed a band concert or a basketball game at our high school. You conveyed to us an understanding of the need for rules in society and the importance of obeying them. Most of all, you gave us a good life during our years in Republic, and for that I thank you fervently.

This will probably be my last letter for a while, Jud. But I won't end it with a goodbye, because I know that I'll be in touch again someday. Besides, we all know how I feel about goodbyes.

With love,

Don

About *Letters to Jud*

This is not a history of Republic, Missouri. It is an account of my time there as I remember it today. All of the tales in these letters are inspired by real events. Some of the events described happened as related, from my experience; others have been expanded and changed. To protect the privacy of persons who may have been involved, some of the individuals portrayed are composites of more than one person, and many names and identifying characteristics have also been changed.

Acknowledgments

Special thanks to editorial, design and publishing consultants at iUniverse for helping make this experience so fulfilling; to Dwayne Mason and Karol Kepchar, intellectual property attorneys, for providing the insightful analysis a project like this requires; to attorney Rick Sdao for his referral; to Ken Scott, of Ken Scott Communications; to Roger McGough, for web page design and maintenance; and to the Republic Historical Society, whose history of Republic helped me to recall certain aspects of my years there.

Why would a man write two dozen letters to a father who has been dead for nearly half a century?

I've done it for two reasons: to finish, at last, some long-unfinished business, and to tell some stories that are too good not to tell.

My father, Judson William Alderman, was a man you might have called unremarkable if you had just met him or knew him only slightly. But if you had known him as I did, you'd have been aware of the special qualities of this modest man who was a railroad depot agent for fifty years—including four hellish years during the Second World War. That railroad, the St. Louis–San Francisco Railway Company, is, like Jud, now also gone.

In his work at the railway depot and at home as a father, he lived in a way that encouraged habits such as industry, fairness, honesty, and dependability. He set those examples naturally, not pedantically. And when his life ended, it ended in a typical, unremarkable, Jud-like way: he just went to sleep one night and didn't wake up.

In some of these letters to Jud, I recall events in which he and my mother, Isabel, were important participants. In others, I confess to activities that I hope they never knew about, for they certainly wouldn't have approved. All of the tales in the letters are based on real events. In some cases, I describe events as they actually happened. In other cases, to protect the privacy of people who might have been involved, I have fictionalized the stories somewhat, created composite characters and used fictional names. I don't tell you when I've done that, because it would be a shame to spoil a good story. The time span covered by these recollections extends from the late 1930s, which is about the time I began to remember things, to the mid-1950s, which is when I left Jud and Isabel to make my own way.

My hope is that these *Letters to Jud* will bring to life a time that can't be replicated in these early years of a new millennium. Perhaps you'll enjoy getting to know my hometown and the warm, wacky, and sometimes tragic people there. They were worth knowing.

* * * * *

I should explain that I did not address my father and mother by their first names during the years that I lived with them. They were "Dad" and "Mom" then. But at some point in my young adult years I began to think of them as Jud and Isabel. That convention may have originated during reunions with my siblings when someone, with good-natured irreverence, would call Dad "Jud" and Mom "Isabel."

There is another, perhaps even more important explanation: In this narrative, I have tried with great affection to portray these two people not just as my parents but as the individuals that they were. I believe that addressing them by first name is important to that goal. Further, I am now older by a decade than Jud was at the end of his life. So, since I now am technically his senior, it should be proper for me to call him by his first name. He'd have agreed with that, I'm certain.

Jud was a month away from his sixty-seventh birthday when he died. I had known him for only twenty-three years, and it seems the time was even shorter than that. All of my memories of Jud are of an older man. He was forty-five years old and Isabel was forty when I was born—along with my twin brother, Bob. They weren't expecting us. In 1933, they thought their family was complete, with three daughters: Jean, age sixteen; Phyllis, ten; and Patricia (Patty), six.

But in the first month of 1934, Jud and Isabel became middle-aged parents of twin boys. In effect, they had to start over and raise a second family. It couldn't have been easy, emotionally or financially. Still, even though Jud's railroad salary was modest, we seemed to live well enough. The few deprivations I can recall were imposed more by World War II than by our family's limited income. Only one disappointment clearly stands out: Jud, a railroad man, never bought us an electric train. When we complained that our friends had model trains, Isabel's response, practical and unarguable as always, was that we didn't need toy trains to play with. We had real ones.

She had a point. As Bob and I grew older, we roamed all around and on top of, if we thought Jud wasn't looking, the boxcars that sat on the tracks near the railroad depot. And when the massive steam locomotives paused in front of the depot, thunking and whooshing wonderfully fragrant clouds of steam from the drive cylinders, we were allowed to stand close enough to smell the hot oil and grease and coal smoke that saturated the air. But we weren't allowed to climb into the engine cab. Nor would Jud let us ride to the town of Billings, Missouri, just four miles from Republic, in the caboose of a freight train. He said that Frisco wasn't paying our family to ride around on their trains. To us, that seemed an unreasonable position for the boss of the railroad station to take.

Eventually, Jud used his railroad pass to give us quite a ride on a Frisco train, and a passenger train at that. In 1943, we took a coach car all the way to St. Louis—250 miles from Republic— to see Stan Musial and the other St. Louis Cardinals play in Sportsman's Park. Ironically, on my first train ride I discovered that I was prone to motion sickness. I was clammy and green by the time we reached the outskirts of St. Louis, and all I could do was gaze weakly into the seedy back yards of homes located along the tracks as our train rolled into the big, strange city. (Thereafter, just a whiff of the musty, cigar-like odor of the interior of a coach or Pullman car triggered nauseating memories of that trip's awful queasiness.)

I quickly recovered from the motion sickness after we stepped from the train, but I felt disconnected from the alien streets and buildings and people I saw on our trolley ride to Sportsman's Park. Once we were in our seats, however, I caught the spirit of the thousands of Cardinals fans who filled the stadium, and I yelled joyfully with them when "Stan the Man" belted one into the right field bleachers.

During my years of active duty with the Naval Reserve, I looked forward to receiving letters from Jud. He wrote eloquently for a man whose formal education ended when he graduated from high school and who thereafter had spent his days working in a railroad station. His writing was clear, straightforward, and, at times, stylish. For many years, he kept a diary in which he recorded thoughts and events that were important to him. During his early years as a father, when the family lived in Ozark, Missouri, Jud described an early morning outing while on a family vacation at a campground:

Sunday, Sept. 20, 1931—Patty, Phyllis and I (Dad) had a date this morning at seven o'clock. Patty was the first one out of bed, and promptly, too. I followed, and as we passed thru Phyl's room, she joined us. Clothes had to be found here and there, but finally, dressing was completed and we started.

The morning was bright with fresh sunshine, the air as warm as mid-summer.

At the park, we all had a good drink of the spring water. After climbing the steps from the spring, we found some children playing with two dogs in front of their cabin. Their parents were hardly out of bed yet. A cage at the cabin door contained two squirrels who continuously ran up one side and down the other. We left the park and walked by Lairs' house. Mr. Lair was leaving for town in his car as we passed.

Now comes the country. The road is along the side of a hill and affords a great view. At the foot of the hill is a field of corn, ripe and ready to be shocked. Close by is a stack of oats and near it a black-and-white bird dog was playing. Across the road that runs parallel in the bottom land is a stack of wheat straw. Beyond are the trees along the banks of the Finley (River) and to the northeast, a glimpse of the lower bridge can be had between the trees. While in the distance, the hills rise on the other side of the valley, revealing fields and orchards and woodlands and a road up the hill, past the farm home near the crest, and down again out of sight.

But a noisy clatter in the sassafras nearby brought our attention close by again. Two blue jays seemed to be quarreling violently; but as we came up, one flew away, thus ending the seeming strife, temporarily at least.

The sun was getting hot and little legs becoming tired. We retraced our footsteps, Phyllis picked some Black-eyed Susans. A mother and restless baby were rocking on Lairs' porch as we returned, and Mrs. Lair, with wash-boiler and pans, informed us she was going to can beans. The people in the cabin were stirring and asked of us the time of day. One of the squirrels paused in its dizzy rounds and, with both front paws, washed its face. We watched with interest. We stopped again at the spring and it took several drinks to quench our thirst. And oh boy, when we got home mama was up and in the kitchen the table was set and breakfast was hot and ready.

I remember Jud as a man who worked long hours at his depot. He usually walked home for lunch and in the evening, after six o'clock, we could expect to see his familiar form walking toward us on Elm Street. During World War II, the demands of heavy rail traffic into and through Republic subjected him to ten- and twelve-hour days, often seven days a week. If there was enough daylight left after supper, he would often seek relief from tension by pushing a hand plow to cultivate our Victory Garden—the name for the gardens in which the government encouraged citizens to grow their own vegetables as part of the war effort. Afterward, he'd smoke his pipe as he sat with Isabel on the front porch after dark.

Bob and I probably didn't understand then, as I do now, that Jud simply had little energy left at the end of his day to spend time with us in father-and-son activities. But even if Jud *had* had more time to share with us—if he hadn't seemed too old to play baseball and basketball with us, or had been more of an outdoorsman, taking us fishing and hunting—I don't know that it would have mattered. He did something else that I began to understand as being very important. He valued the quiet, quality times of his life. He noted them and savored the details and stored them away. And in his quiet way, he taught me to do that, too.

After graduating from the University of Houston, where he studied journalism and creative writing, Don Alderman began his long career as an advertising agency copywriter, creative director, agency principal and financial services writer. He and his wife, Colleen, live in Houston and have four children.